D1137428

My Mum and the Green-eyed Monster

'I was hoping for a quiet patch. Fat chance! The last two years in our house have been like living in a soap opera – except no one would believe the script!'

Kate is thunderstruck when Belle – the family's attractive new au pair – charms everyone, including Kate's so-called best friend, Chas. Worse, Chas seems to have forgotten Kate in his new skateboarding craze. She is seething with jealousy and confusion, when tragedy strikes…

Meg Harper divides her days between writing, teaching drama and running round after her four teenagers! In her spare time, she enjoys reading, swimming, walking her dog and visiting tea-shops with friends. Occasionally, she escapes it all by becoming a Tudor basket maker at re-enactments.

Other titles in this series: *My Mum and Other Horror Stories*, *My Mum and the Gruesome Twosome* and *My Mum and the Hound from Hell*.

3 4114 00357 8993

For Su, who believed the first
'My Mum' book would work.
With huge thanks for being my editor.

My Mum
and the
Green-eyed
Monster

Meg Harper

LION
Children's Books

BLACKPOOL LIBRARIES	
00357899	
Bertrams	11.02.06
	£4.99

Text copyright © 2006 Meg Harper
This edition copyright © 2006 Lion Hudson

The moral rights of the author
have been asserted

A Lion Children's Book
an imprint of
Lion Hudson plc
Mayfield House, 256 Banbury Road,
Oxford OX2 7DH, England
www.lionhudson.com
ISBN-13: 978 0 7459 4993 2
ISBN-10: 0 7459 4993 2

First edition 2006
10 9 8 7 6 5 4 3 2 1 0

All rights reserved

A catalogue record for this book is available
from the British Library

Typeset in 11/16 Garamond ITC Light BT
Printed and bound in Great Britain
by Cox and Wyman Ltd, Reading

Contents

1   My Mum and the Awful Au Pair   7

2   My Mum and the Skaters   22

3   My Mum's Dog's Dinner   36

4   My Mum and Mrs Charming Peterson   51

5   My Mum and Gran   64

6   My Mum and the Awful Au Pair – Again!   78

7   My Mum and the Party   91

8   My Mum Rescues Greg   107

9   My Mum Gets to Be Famous   117

10   My Mum Sorts Me Out   129

11   My Mum is Right in the End... as Usual.   139

1

My Mum and the Awful Au Pair

What did I do wrong? Why me? Why did I have to get stuck in a family that's way too weird to function in a normal watch-TV-mow-the-lawn-go-shopping sort of way? Sometimes I wonder why God doesn't just wipe us out and start again! Can't say I'd blame him if he did.

He could start with our new au pair, Belle. It's because of her that I'm stuck here in my bedroom 'cooling off' as Mum puts it. She's been here less than a week and we are sworn enemies already. I just went to have a nice relaxing bath and what did I find? She'd used up all my special mango bubble bath that my best friend Chas gave me. I stormed off downstairs to find her.

'You've used up all my bubble bath!' I started.

'Excuse me, Kate! I am watching a programme,' she said.

'No, I won't "excuse you",' I said. 'When I let you borrow it on the day you arrived, I didn't mean you could go on using it day after day! It was a present!'

'Well, I am sorry. I did not understand.'

'Well, you do now,' I raged, 'so I'd quite like it if you bought me a new bottle, please!'

'I cannot afford a new bottle, Kate,' said Belle. 'Au pairs do not get paid very much, you know.'

It was at this moment that Mum came in. She was supposed to be getting my twin baby sisters ready for bed.

'Kate, what's all the noise for?' she asked. 'I can hear you upstairs. The girls will never go to sleep at this rate!'

'It's Belle,' I fumed. 'She's used up all my mango bubble bath and she won't buy me a new bottle!' I saw the expression on Mum's face and could have kicked myself. I knew what I sounded like – a spoilt baby.

'I am sorry, Jo,' said Belle. 'I misunderstood. I thought Kate did not mind if I used her bubble bath.'

'I meant once!' I snarled. 'Just once, on your first day here.'

'Kate, you're making rather a fuss,' said Mum. 'It was an easy mistake to make. Belle's English isn't perfect, you know.'

'It is when she wants it to be,' I muttered. 'Like when she's chatting up boys.'

'I heard that,' said Mum, 'and it was very rude and uncalled for. Now apologize to Belle, please. At once.'

'No,' I said. 'You're being completely unfair! She ought to say sorry to me for using all my bubble bath!'

'Well, if you won't apologize, I will for you,' said Mum. 'I *do* apologize, Belle, for the rudeness of my daughter. And you, Kate, had better go to your room until you've cooled off.'

Well! How's that for injustice? I couldn't believe it. There's definitely something funny about Mum at the moment. How can she be so taken in?

I was hoping for a quiet patch. Fat chance! The last two years in our house have been like living in a soap opera – except no one would believe the script. Normal families don't have mothers who fracture their skulls, give birth to twins and adopt mad dogs, while supposedly working part-time as cool vicars with funky, multi-coloured hair, thanks to their hairdresser husbands. I suppose some other families do have batty grannies who keep escaping from nursing homes but I bet they never employ hunky, male, cello-playing au pairs or have twelve-year-old sons who already have steady girlfriends and use anti-spot face packs!

But my family does. We make The Addams Family look well adjusted. OK, so I'm in a Wednesday Addams mood, I admit it. I've got the evils and that's why I'm sitting here at my computer, battering my long-suffering keyboard. Stops me from storming downstairs and scratching out a certain someone's make-up-plastered eyes!

A quiet patch! Huh! For weeks I was in agony because Chas got packed off to boarding school (thanks to his snobby mother, Mrs Oh-So-Charming Peterson). He ran away (he's not stupid) so I've had a couple of months of relative peace. Chas is back at my school, mad dog Rover has begun to behave himself and my twin baby sisters have finally understood the difference between day and night – well, mostly. (Yes, darlings, night-time is when we go to *sleep*!)

Then – thunderbolt! Our lovely, lovely au pair Nic (OK so it took me a while to get used to having a bloke wandering round the house smelling of baby powder and singing lullabies) had to leave! He's a fantastic cellist and he was offered the chance to fill in for another musical genius who had an accident. He'll tour with this string quartet for a few months and then start university later in the year. It's a great opportunity so he couldn't possibly turn it down – but that's why we've got stuck with the appalling Belle.

Dad says I'm being unreasonable and should give her a chance. He has tactlessly pointed out on several occasions that I wasn't too keen on Nic when he first arrived. (That was different. How was I to know that, far from being the sort of male moron who pees all over the loo floor and never puts the milk back in the fridge, Nic was better house-trained than mad dog Rover?) Anyway, I am certainly not keen on Belle. I'm not keen on Belle like I'm not keen on arsenic in tea, cyanide in sandwiches or bleach sprinkled on my chips. She is *poison*.

'But she's very attractive,' says little brother Ben, who has been all raging boy hormones for the last year. And Chas, the disloyal skunk, agrees! It wouldn't be so bad but she's so *obvious*! She certainly knows what to do with a Wonderbra and mascara. And as for that sexy French accent, I'm sure she puts it on deliberately. Her English is *sooo* perfect (whatever Mum says), I can't believe she couldn't manage the accent if she tried. Yes, very attractive, I'm sure. Like Deadly

Nightshade is attractive. For which the Latin name is, as it happens, *Belladonna*. So that's what I've decided to call her. Belladonna. Ha!

Dad overheard me one day and had a right old go at me about it.

'So?' I said. 'She doesn't even know what it means, so what does it matter? She probably thinks it's a compliment.'

'Hmm…' said Dad, giving me the worldy-wise smile he thinks is so irresistible. He doesn't know I'm proof against it these days. 'Now what does it say in the Bible? "The Lord detests lying lips but he delights in those who are truthful."'

That's another of the mega weird things about my parents. They have a handy little Bible verse to trot out for every occasion. Seems fair enough for a part-time vicar – but a *hairdresser*? I wonder if he does it to his customers? 'Your hair is like royal tapestry.' That's from the Song of Songs. I'm not sure I'd take it as a compliment. Anyway, sometimes what the parents come up with is really useful but sometimes it's just very, very annoying.

'So?' I countered. 'You think I should tell her the truth? That I think she's horrible and the sooner she goes back to France the better?'

Dad sighed. 'No, I'm just suggesting that you give her a chance. She's only been here a few days and you've decided you hate her already. It's not *her* fault she's so pretty.'

'Oh no, not you too,' I said, disgusted. 'Don't you think you're a bit old for her, Dad? That she might think your grey Francis Rossi ponytail is a bit last century?'

Dad sighed again. 'Oh, grow up, Kate,' he said. 'If you're feeling that bad, why don't you go and start that computer journal of yours again? That way none of the rest of us will have to listen to your vitriol.'

Vitriol. Nice word. I looked it up. It means caustic speech or feeling. A good Wednesday Addams word. I shall remember it.

Maybe I'd be coping better with Belladonna if she seemed a bit more useful. So far it seems she hardly does a thing. She wouldn't do anything which involved getting her hands wet until we'd got her some rubber gloves because she has 'extra-sensitive skin'. And the first time she had to change a dirty nappy, she nearly had a fit. Mum's still breastfeeding the twins a lot so the contents weren't quite what Belle expected. She thought there was something seriously wrong with Rebekah and started screaming for help. Ben and I came running to find her brandishing the nappy in one hand, pinning a howling Rebekah to the changing mat with the other and babbling away about calling the doctor. Ben grabbed the nappy and I quickly sorted out Rebekah and calmed her down.

'It's quite all right, Belle,' said Ben. 'That's perfectly normal, honestly.'

Belle gaped at Ben as if he was raving mad and squawked, 'But... but... it's yellow!'

'It's fine,' said Ben, looking as strong and manly as he could manage. 'Believe me, baby poo is meant to be like that.'

Then Belle (and this will really make you puke) fluttered

her heavily mascara-ed lashes (waterproof, of course) and elegantly burst into soul-shuddering sobs. She could have been on film.

'I am *so* sorry,' she gulped. 'I have never changed a baby's nappy before.'

Ben was taken in, of course, and ended up making her a cup of tea 'for the shock'. She couldn't lift a finger for at least half an hour. So 'experienced with babies' on her au pair agency form actually meant 'have experienced the *nice* bits of babies'. Grrr!

It wouldn't be so bad but Mum really doesn't need this sort of grief at the moment. I'm worried about her. She's always been so full of energy. Even when she was pregnant with the twins, there was hardly any stopping her. It used to be one project after another – belly-dancing, abseiling, bungee jumping – you name it, she was up for it. We narrowly escaped having her keep a pig in the garden and mad dog Rover was definitely another of her 'projects' even though *I* got dragged along to the training classes. Mum drives me bonkers half the time but she's always had a great sense of humour. We used to call her Big Bum Mum (boy, has she got one!), Big Tum Mum (when she was pregnant) and then Big Dumb Mum (when she adopted Rover) and she's always had a laugh about it. But now she's Big Glum Mum and I daren't let her hear me say it. She's more likely to cry than to laugh. It's like she's a big party balloon that's gradually losing all its helium and is just drifting at the end of its string. Dad thinks she should go to the doctor. Everyone knows that some women get really down when they've had a baby – and she's had two! But she says, 'I'm not depressed, I'm just tired. I'll be fine when Hayley and Comet sleep through the night.' That just shows she's not herself. Comet's real name is Rebekah but when the twins were born Halley's Comet was in the news. Mum always jumps on us for calling Rebekah Comet; if she's started to join in, that's bad!

Meanwhile, the last thing she needs is a silly, simpering au pair who doesn't like getting her hands dirty and doesn't know one end of a baby from the other. Every nappy she puts on leaks or falls off and if she picks either twin up, you can guarantee it'll be crying two minutes later. And Mum is so patient! If it were me, I'd have packed Belle off back where she came from before you could say baby-puke. Mum says a new au pair needs time to settle in and it was easier for Nic because he had the chance to learn the ropes before the twins were born. Patience isn't Mum's strong suit so that's worrying too. It's more like she can't be bothered to do anything about it. If she were her normal self, she wouldn't be putting up with this. Belladonna would be back home by now – wherever that festering bog happens to be!

She's got to go! She's simply got to go! I know the Bible blahs on about loving your enemies and being welcoming to strangers and aliens (Question: does that mean the *Star Trek* sort?) but surely there are limits?

Last night, Belladonna went to a party. Of course, to hear her whingeing on, you'd think she had the social life of a bag lady.

All her friends have exciting jobs in London, where life is one long party but all *her* money goes on essentials like hair dyeing (with discount from Dad), leg waxing, nail polishing and eyelash extending. Poor little Cinders has to sit at home and suffer, reading horrible, boring magazines and soaking in nasty, slimy mango-scented bubble baths. In fact, it took her just one day on the local college's English course to give her mobile number to the entire male population and when it rings, she simply has to answer it. How my heart bleeds for her!

Anyway, last night's bash was a jolly good excuse for her not to be available to clear up after tea or help with the babies' bedtime routine. She actually had the cheek to hammer on the bathroom door and ask when it would be free as she was in a bit of a hurry! Finally, she was swept away by a creepy-looking guy on a motorbike and we all breathed a sigh of relief. Oh, all right – I breathed a sigh of relief and the rest jolly well ought to have done.

At two in the morning, the phone rang. Mum and Dad sleep like the dead in between bouts of baby-feeding – it's a newly learned survival tactic – but the ringing woke me so I staggered downstairs. With Gran being as frail as she is, I was dreading it being some awful news about her. My hand was shaking as I lifted the receiver and mumbled our number.

'Who is that?' asked a peremptory voice.

'It's Kate Lofthouse. Is that the nursing home?'

'No. What are you talking about?'

My fuggy brain recognized the accent. 'Bellado... Belle? Is that you?' I gasped.

'Yes, of course it is. I am stuck at this party and I need a lift home.'

I was so flabbergasted I couldn't speak for a moment.

'Kate? Are you there? I said I need a lift home. Please tell your father or mother to come to get me.'

'What's happened to the bloke who took you?' I asked. 'Aren't you coming home with him?'

Belle gave a disgusted snort. 'He cannot drive anyone anywhere,' she said. 'He has drunk too much of your awful English beer. One of your parents must collect me.'

I was so furious I nearly slammed the phone down. Didn't she understand what she was here for? Did she need it spelling out? Hadn't she realized that having twins means sleep deprivation and an au pair is supposed to help with that, not add to it?

'Just where are you?' I demanded. 'Can't you get a taxi?'

'Of course not,' said Belladonna. 'I cannot afford one. Please go to get one of your parents.'

'They're both asleep,' I said, narrowly avoiding tagging 'you idiot' on the end. 'Can't you borrow some money from someone?'

'No. I would need about twenty-five pounds.'

'Twenty-five pounds? Where on earth are you?'

'I think the town is called Bicester. It took about half an hour to get here.'

I could hardly believe what I was hearing. Did she seriously think it was all right for Mum or Dad to go and get her in the middle of the night when she was half an hour away? Even five minutes would be bad enough!

'How about sleeping on the sofa?' I suggested. 'You could come back in the morning on the train.'

'Sleep on the sofa? Kate, you must be mad! How would I sleep on the sofa?'

'Try lying on it,' I snapped and then I really did slam the phone down. I was so angry that my legs were shaking and I slumped to the floor. Rover, who has his basket in the hall, lifted his head and gave me a reproachful look. The phone rang again immediately. I snatched it up.

'Go away!' I shouted and slammed it down again. I was just about to take it off the hook when I heard someone shuffling across the landing. Dad appeared at the top of the stairs.

'What's going on, Kate?' he asked.

The phone rang again. I picked it up and covered the mouthpiece while I spoke to him.

'It's Belladonna,' I hissed. 'She wants a lift home from *Bicester*.'

Dad's eyebrows shot up but he staggered down the stairs and took the receiver from me.

'Go back to bed, Kate,' he said. 'I'll sort it out.'

'Don't you dare give her a lift,' I said, refusing to budge.

'I'll do what I think is right, Kate,' said Dad in a voice that could have frozen boiling oil.

It was cold in the hall and I didn't have my bathrobe. Fury had been keeping me warm but the effect was wearing off. Reluctantly, I mounted the stairs. I was wide awake and far too angry to sleep but I knew that if I stood there shivering,

Dad would get mad with me. It was obvious he was going to give in, whether I stood there glaring at him or not.

Huddling under my duvet, I heard Dad return to his room, a murmured exchange with Mum and the clink of his car keys. I swore under my breath, felt bad about it and then blamed Belladonna. Honestly, she'd drive a saint to swear.

I was still awake when she and Dad returned nearly an hour later. It must have been getting on for four when I finally drifted into an uneasy sleep and dreamed of poisonous weeds taking over the bathroom. Very Wednesday.

To cap that, this morning, Belladonna simply *had* to sleep in. When I tottered blearily into the bathroom for a shower, she had the nerve to hammer on the wall and shout at me to be quiet!

I was not in the best of tempers when I finally hit the kitchen and was unimpressed to find Chas and Ben having a toast fest. I knew I looked rotten in my grubby old bathrobe and the sight of Chas, cool, clean and casual, didn't improve my mood.

'You'll never believe what Belladonna did last night!' I said, brushing aside toast crumbs to make space for my breakfast – boys are such slobs!

'We've heard,' said Chas. 'Bet your dad wasn't very pleased – but these things happen.'

'These things happen!' I spat. 'What d'you mean? These things happen?'

'Well, what was she supposed to do?' asked Ben. 'She was

expecting that bloke to bring her back and he let her down. She could hardly stay at the party all night.'

I stared at him so incredulously that I'm surprised my eyes didn't fall out of their sockets.

'Yes she could,' I snapped. 'Have you never heard of the concept of sleepovers?'

'Yeah, obviously – but she's French, isn't she?' said Ben.

'So? And your point is? You think the French still live like last century? All guillotines and fancy wigs?'

'That was a couple of centuries ago, actually, Kate,' said Chas, with a grin.

'You know what I mean!' I raged. 'Typical! You're so taken with her bella bella boobs and her bellissimo butt that you can't see that she's a manipulative little piece of pondweed!'

'Bella and bellissimo are Italian, Kate,' said Chas.

'And Belladonna doesn't grow in ponds,' added Ben.

I was just drawing myself up to my full height to let rip when I saw their exchange of glances.

'You... you toerags!' I burst out. 'Stop trying to wind me up!'

They collapsed in pathetic giggles.

'Oh Kate,' snorted Chas. 'It's just too easy! Lighten up. Have some breakfast.'

'Yeah, what's it to you anyway?' chuntered Ben. 'It was Dad who went and got her, not you – and *he* couldn't have a lie-in to recover. He's gone to the salon, same as usual.'

'You little creep!' I snapped, still irritated. 'It wasn't you that got up to answer the phone at two in the morning, was it?'

Ben shrugged. 'Can I help it if I sleep like a log?'

The outside door opened and BGM backed in holding Rover, who promptly escaped and bounded over to Chas to tell him how thrilling it was to see him. I hoped he slavered all over his pristine jeans. Right then, I wasn't as enchanted with him as the mad mutt was.

'Can anyone help me get the twins out of the buggy?' BGM asked. The babies, still outside and strapped in their seats, were already beginning to squirm and grizzle. 'I don't suppose Belle's around, is she?'

'Too right,' I said, standing up. 'No – don't trouble yourself, boys. Don't feel the need to leave your toast. I know you're only on your tenth slice. The unpaid skivvy will help.'

If Mum was up to her usual form she wouldn't have let me get away with that bit of nastiness, but she just shrugged and handed Comet to me. We were both busily removing the twins' hats and jackets when Belladonna breezed in, radiant from her bath.

'Ah, Belle,' said Mum, smiling at her. 'Would you just bring the double buggy in and fold it away for me, please?'

Belle's shoulders sagged. 'May I have my breakfast first, please?' she asked.

'Don't worry,' said Ben, leaping up. 'I'll do it.'

'Toast?' grunted Chas, blushing.

Belle perched herself complacently on a stool. 'Oh yes please,' she said with a demure little dip of her luscious lashes.

I plonked Comet on her lap. If you do these things fast

enough, you can get away with them. Even Belladonna isn't evil enough to drop a baby – I hope.

'Sorry everyone,' I said. 'Must dash – I think I'm going to be sick. It must be because I'm overtired.'

I took a moment to enjoy Belladonna's disgusted expression – there was definitely something noxious lurking in Comet's nappy – and then I marched out of the room. Touché!

2

My Mum and the Skaters

It's remarkable what writing a journal can do for you; I felt so much better after I'd poured out all that vitriol (my new word) about Belle's party stunt. I'm hoping it'll work its magic now; I'm feeling very Wednesday-ish!

This morning, I decided to be kind to animals (not little brother Ben, in this case, though he does qualify) and take Rover for a long walk. Chas lives on a farm about three miles away so that was the obvious destination. He doesn't do much on a Saturday unless we've arranged something together, sometimes with my friend Vicky, sometimes with Ben and his girlfriend Suzie, sometimes just me and him on our own. I expected he'd just be reading in his den (this old outhouse where he's allowed to make as much mess as he wants and keeps several cats) or playing some boring old computer game or other. He cycles to school so he's not a complete slob – in fact, he's the sort that wouldn't put on weight even if he lived on a diet of chips and chocolate – but he's not exactly the sporty type. Or that's what I thought until today.

I walked quickly because it was cold and damp. Rover didn't care of course. He was just thrilled to be out and about. Once we'd got into the countryside, I turned onto a footpath where I could let him off his lead. I used to be absolutely terrified that he'd run amok and get shot for sheep-worrying but he's turning out to be a sensible, well-behaved dog now. Mum claims it's all the hours we've put into his dog training but I have this feeling he's a pretty clever young mutt really. If it wasn't for him, Chas could have ended up crumpled at the bottom of a small cliff not all that long ago. The great thing is that I feel so much safer walking on my own, now that we have Rover. He's big and black and hairy. He's a softy really but your average mad axeman isn't to know that.

When we got to Chas's house, I didn't go to the front door as Rover was very muddy. You might not think that would be a problem on a farm but I assure you, it is! Chas's dad is the estate manager rather than an ordinary farmer, so the house the Petersons live in isn't the actual farmhouse. In fact, it's Mrs Charming Peterson's very own show home. It would feature nicely in an article in *Country Life* magazine or *Homes and Gardens*. Rover once puked all over the designer hearth rug so I avoid taking him in if I can.

Anyway, I didn't want to see Mrs Charming Peterson, I wanted to see Chas, so I went straight over to his den, knocked and opened the door.

'Chas!' I called as I kicked off my wellies. 'It's me. Have you got a rag or something I can rub Rover down with?'

No reply. I expected Chas to be glued to his computer, lost in some ridiculous fantasy world of muscular heroes and Lara Croft-ettes, so I wasn't exactly surprised. (Question: do boys actually lose the power of speech and hearing when playing computer games or do they just pretend?)

'Chas!' I called again. 'Wakey, wakey! Have you got an old towel?'

Nothing.

Boys! Honestly! With five minutes to live, what would you do? 'Oh... errr... I'll just finish this level...'

But Chas wasn't just finishing this level. He wasn't there.

I confess, I was surprised and a bit hurt. It's not like I expect to know his every move or anything, it's just that since he's come back from that awful boarding school, we've spent nearly all our free time together one way or another. I hadn't said I'd definitely pop round but I just thought he might be expecting me. It was possible that he'd been dragged off by his dad to do some useful job on the estate so I rummaged around and found a very old sweatshirt (a cat seemed to have adopted it as a bed) and rubbed Rover down with that. Then I found one of Chas's endless supply of Terry Pratchett books and sat down to wait.

It was a good book and Rover was happily (if naughtily) snuggled up beside me on the beaten-up old sofa, so I didn't notice the time passing until I began to feel hungry. Strange. Where on earth could Chas be? Sometimes he gets marched off to see relatives at the weekend but not much these days – that's the sort of thing parents tend to give up on once you're a teenager, thank goodness – and anyway, both cars had been in the yard when I arrived. It was unlikely that Chas was in the house; he spends as little time in there as possible. Even so, I decided I would go and check. I'd had a pleasant hour or so reading but really I wanted to see Chas.

'Stay here,' I told Rover. 'Don't chase the cats.' He thumped his tail and grinned at me, then snuggled his nose between his paws. He wouldn't bother the cats unless they bothered him; he was far too comfortable.

I hurried across the yard and banged the brass knocker which, I was surprised to notice, was slightly less bright and gleaming than usual. The door swung open.

'Kate! Darling!' Mrs Peterson gushed. 'You haven't come up to see Chas, have you?'

'Well, yes, I have actually. Isn't he here?'

'Oh dear, he's gone off with some friends to one of these big skateparks – there's some sort of competition on, I think.'

'Skateparks?' I said, bemused. 'For skateboarders? Chas?'

'Yes. He's suddenly got very interested in skateboarding – I've no idea why. He sprang this competition on us this morning. One of his friends could give him a lift there if we could give him and the rest of them a lift back.'

'But... but...' I stammered, 'Chas hasn't even got a skateboard!'

'No, but apparently he's been having a go on someone else's. He tells me he's a natural. He's going to get a skateboard today. There'll be a big sale at the competition and he should be able to get one for a good price.'

I gaped at her.

'I was surprised too, Kate. It quite took the wind out of my sails. I just hope he's not going to grow his hair long and wear one of those awful caps. But then, boys will be boys, I suppose – and it's good healthy exercise, out in the fresh air.'

I couldn't think what to say. Chas? Into skateboarding? And he'd never so much as mentioned it to me? I couldn't believe it. Was I speaking to the right mother?

'So what time will he be back?' I asked, at last.

'Well, I'm not quite sure, actually. He was a bit vague about that – he didn't seem to know when the competition would finish. He said he'd ring when he knew what time I should collect him.' Mrs Peterson gave her tinkly little laugh. 'I don't know – wanting a bit of freedom, I should think. I can't tie him to my apron strings forever.'

I felt like slapping my face to see if I woke up. The world was changing too fast for me. Mrs Peterson? Fussy, gushy, overprotective Mrs Peterson, laughing about not knowing what time her precious son would be back? Was this the same woman who'd packed Chas off to boarding school because she didn't think he was mixing with the right people and was worried about exam results?

'Err… well, could you ask him to phone me when he gets in?' I said. 'I guess there's no point in waiting.'

'Of course I will, Kate. Now we'd better see about getting you home. Give me a minute and we'll sort out a lift.'

'Oh, I've got Rover with me,' I gabbled. 'We'll be fine walking!'

'Nonsense, Kate! Look at that sky. Any minute now, it's going to pour with rain. You'll get soaked. Go and get Rover; he can travel in the boot. Hurry now, there's a good girl!'

I was too gob-smacked to argue. Five minutes later, I'd been steamrollered into the Land Rover and was on my way home. To my surprise, it was Mr Peterson who took me; he's a very quiet man so I didn't have to make conversation which was just as well. I was shocked into brain meltdown. Chas? Skateboarding? And without saying anything to me, his best friend? What on earth was going on?

Mrs Charming had been right about the weather. We'd just got to my house when rain started lashing down. I ran for the cover of our porch, wondering how Chas was enjoying himself at the skateboard competition and trying not to be glad that he was probably getting drenched.

At about four o'clock, the phone rang. I'd given up on finding any entertainment for the day – Vicky had been dragged off to tea at her uncle's so I was half-heartedly doing my homework. I snatched up the receiver, glad of the break.

It was Mrs Charming Peterson but she sounded unusually harassed and anxious.

'Is your mum there, Kate?' she asked. 'I wonder if I could ask her to do me a favour?'

This was very odd. Mrs Charming is convinced that Mum has far too much on her plate and is forever doing *her* favours

– ringing up to ask if any shopping needs doing, bringing round a plate of scones or a casserole when she's been cooking, offering to babysit for a couple of hours. What on earth could she want Mum to do?

I called her anyway and told her who it was.

'Right, Kate, off you go then,' she said, taking the phone from me.

I stared at her. What was the hurry? It was only Mrs Charming, not some desperate member of the church congregation ringing up to cry on her shoulder.

'Go on,' said Mum, flapping a hand at me. 'Leave me in peace, please.'

Slowly, because I objected to being bossed about like that, I went into the sitting room. Then, bursting with curiosity, I glued my ear to the door.

Much good it did me. It was a quick conversation, I could hardly hear anything and when Mum pulled the door open, it was pretty hard to jump back quickly and pretend I was reading a book. Fortunately, Mum had too much on her mind to notice.

'I don't know,' she said, bustling in. 'Your Chas is turning into a real pain. He's been driving his mum mad since he came home from that boarding school; she's wishing she'd sent him back.'

'Shouldn't have sent him in the first place,' I said. 'He was fine before he went.'

'Rubbish, Kate – he's just being a typical teenage boy. I hope Ben doesn't go like he's gone – all grunting and skateboards. And he's refusing to have a haircut – wants to grow it long like those professional skateboarders do.'

I'd noticed that and rather liked it. With his soulful eyes and lean body, Chas was beginning to look vaguely like Johnny Depp.

'Is that what she rang about?' I asked. 'She sounded a bit stressed.'

'No, she wants to know if I can go and pick him up from this skatepark. She's not feeling well and her husband's busy on the farm somewhere. It has to be someone with a big car because he's got a gang of friends with him.'

Friends? Was Chas calling that gang of skateboarding losers friends now? It was news to me!

'So are you going?' I asked, surprised. 'She seemed fine when I was up there earlier on.'

'Of course I'm going!' Mum said. 'I was hoping you'd come too, to read the map. This place sounds a bit difficult to find.'

'What about the babies?' I said.

'Belle will have to look after them; this is a crisis.'

I snorted. I could just imagine what Belle would say to that.

I was right. No surprises there.

'But Saturday is my day off,' she protested from her bed, where she was lying, re-painting her finger nails.

'I'm sorry, Belle, I'll have to let you have the time off later in the week,' said Mum. 'Right now, we need to get off to Birmingham, so if you could just come downstairs quickly, I'll explain what needs to happen.'

'But I haven't finished my nails,' said Belle. 'Can't you take the babies with you?'

Mum sighed. 'No, Belle, I can't,' she said. 'I think I've explained to you that if they travel in the car at this time of day, they fall asleep and then won't go to bed later. In any case, it would take ten minutes to get them ready. Please just come downstairs.'

'I'll be five minutes,' said Belle woodenly.

Ten minutes later, we were still waiting. Just when I was about to tell Mum what a waste of space she was, Belle appeared, looking immaculate but grumpy.

'Now then, Belle, we shouldn't be more than a couple of hours,' said Mum. 'If the girls start whining, make them some toast fingers and Marmite. That should keep them going till I get back. And Ben should be in soon. I'm sure he won't mind helping.'

I felt like saying that he shouldn't have to help – what were we paying Belladonna for? – but thought the better of it. Mum looked stressed and tired enough as it was; I didn't want a scene.

It took a long time to find the skatepark. Mrs Charming's directions weren't brilliant and she'd missed out one roundabout, which sent us badly astray. By the time we finally got there, Mum was thoroughly steamed up. In a way, I was quite glad – she's been so droopy and lacklustre recently that it was reassuring to see her bristling with impatience. When the boys weren't waiting at the entrance, however, my alarm bells began to ring. Mum was already worrying about being much longer than she'd said she would be; I could see things getting nasty.

'I'll try Chas on my mobile,' I said before Mum could start complaining. The fact that I have a mobile at all is one of the things that has got me worried about Mum. She's convinced they fry your brain and give you cancer so wouldn't let me have one for ages. Then, suddenly, not very long ago, she gave in. There didn't seem to be a reason – just that she couldn't be bothered to argue any more. It's not exactly all-singing, all-dancing, of course, but at least it phones and sends texts.

Chas's phone was turned off. 'Plonker,' I muttered and then left a message. It looked like we were going to have to search the park.

It took us a good ten minutes to find Chas and his posse, by which time Mum looked ready to knock their heads together.

'Oh, hi!' said Chas. 'Is it time to go?'

'Just move,' I hissed. 'Before Mum kills you! You should have been at the gate waiting.'

'Oh sorry,' grunted Chas. 'Lost track of the time. Come on you lot. Our lift's here.'

A ragtag bunch of boys in black T-shirts and baseball caps followed us to the car. They didn't say 'hi', they didn't say 'sorry', they just grunted at each other and chewed gum.

Please don't let her start a scene, God, I muttered under my breath. I'll die if she starts a scene.

Chas seemed to be ignoring me completely. I had hoped when I'd agreed to help Mum find the park that it would give me a chance to talk to him. Now I was kicking myself for being so stupid. Even if he was still my best friend (and he had me worried), he was hardly going to talk to me in front of this bunch. There were blokes at school who liked me but not this lot. I was 'that vicar's kid' as far as they were concerned – a real loser. If Chas was going to be a skater from now on, where did that leave me? I couldn't believe it. When he'd been away at school he'd got all grumpy and jealous because he thought I didn't care that he'd gone. We'd sorted that out – and now he was treating me like he didn't want to know me! Had he turned into an oik overnight?

I got in the front of the car with Mum and Chas and his mates got in the back. They still hadn't spoken to either of us but were soon grunting at each other like a sty full of surly pigs. I concentrated hard to understand what they were saying but all I could hear was stuff about 'ollieing stair sets' and 'getting air on halfpipes'.

'Oh gosh!' said one of them suddenly. 'Look at my flippin' deck! It's cracked! That was you, Jase, you flippin' idiot!'

I have politely written 'gosh', 'flippin'' and 'idiot' because those words roughly approximate to what he meant. The words he actually used, I can't write down. They were far too rude.

Mum swerved the car into the side of the road and slammed on the brakes, causing the man behind to honk his horn loudly.

'What happened?' said one of the boys. 'Is something wrong?' Good grief, it can speak English! I thought.

Mum said nothing but got out of the car, walked round to the pavement and opened the sliding door.

'Out!' she said. 'All of you! Yes, you too, Chas. No, I'm not joking. Get out of my car now! Kate, stay where you are!'

I buried my head in my hands and tried to pretend I didn't exist. I'm going to die, I thought. This time, I really, really am going to die of embarrassment.

I peered through my fingers into the wing mirror and could just see that Mum had got the boys lined up on the pavement as if she was about to make them hold out their hands for a caning. Instead, she marched up and down the rank of damp, dismal looking creatures and ranted at them. I was glad she'd shut the door so I couldn't hear what she was saying but I could guess. Bad manners and swearing don't go down very well with BGM, especially when she's tired and stressed. Finally, she let them all back into the car. They were suitably silent. Then, one of them was stupid enough to giggle. For one horrible moment, I thought she would have them back out on the pavement again. Instead, she said, in a voice that made Godzilla sound friendly, 'One more giggle or swear word and I'll drop you all off at the station and you can get the train back home. Don't think I don't mean it.'

They got the picture. Our car was as silent as the grave for the rest of the trip back to Banbury, where the boys were being picked up. I shrank into my seat and hoped they'd forget I was there or had any connection with the tyrant in the driver's seat.

BGM hadn't finished however. As soon as she'd got rid of his friends, Mum started on Chas.

'I have never… your mother would be ashamed… when I think of what we've done… you used to be… blah, blah, blah.' I shut my eyes tight and tried to pretend it wasn't happening. Hot tears seeped through my lashes but I knuckled them away. I could see Mum's point of view – she had been very supportive when Chas ran away from boarding school – but she was going completely over the top. Chas has always liked her. He'd hate her after this! Ever since he first got to know us, he's treated our house like a second home. How would he feel now?

Mum only stopped ranting when she was driving into the farmyard. Chas opened the door to get out. For one awful moment, I thought he wasn't going to thank her. Fortunately, he did.

'Thanks for the lift,' he said. 'We really appreciated it.' Mum visibly relaxed and managed the glimmer of a smile. Then Chas blew it. 'I'm sorry it's put you in such a bad mood.'

'Well!' gasped Mum and I thought she was going to leap out of the car and strangle him on the spot. But Chas had gone, sprinting off for the den before she could move.

'Leave it, please, Mum,' I begged. 'The babies will be wanting you.'

'Huh!' said Mum. 'Well, at least they're grateful for the efforts I make!'

All the way home, I prayed that Belle would have managed to keep the babies happy. Unbelievably, she had. She had them sitting in their high chairs chomping away on Marmite soldiers. For the very first time, I felt some warmth towards her; I couldn't have faced more awfulness at home.

Belle seemed to be glowing with her own success. 'Jo, you look very tired,' she said. 'Would you like me to make you a cup of tea?'

Amazing! Welcome to the age of miracles!

3

My Mum's Dog's Dinner

I lay awake last night, worrying. It's not like I have no friends. Apart from Chas, there's Vicky. We've had our moments, of course. She got really stressed with me when we both fancied Gorgeous (re-named Grotty) Greg but she was still a real help when Chas went off to boarding school and things began to go wrong between him and me. And there are other people who like me – girls I play tennis with, friends from church and kids I sit next to in lessons. But somehow, if things go wrong with Chas, I feel really out of sorts. We've had some big ups and downs in our friendship but I had thought we'd got things on an even keel for now. Considering the fuss he made about me appearing to forget about him when he went to boarding school, you'd have thought I was his one true love – except that he's never so much as kissed me! I could get really cross with him, actually. I mean, he was *so* stressy because he thought I fancied Greg (well, I did, for a while) and was ignoring him but now he's gone and got himself stuck into this skateboarding crew without even mentioning it! Sounds like one rule for him and a different one for me. I think I'll try and catch him at church and see if he'll tell me more about it.

Chas wasn't at church! His mum and dad were but not him. Why on earth not? I was determined to find out so I went marching up to Mrs Charming Peterson to demand an explanation.

'Oh yes, I know, he *is* being naughty, isn't he?' said Mrs C, looking guilty. 'He said he was really tired after yesterday and that he'd got so much homework to do that he'd better stay at home. I said you'd miss him.'

My jaw dropped open in amazement. Mrs Charming Peterson has always been a no-nonsense sort of woman; that's probably why she and BGM get on so well. And here she was throwing in the towel at the first opportunity!

She could see that I wasn't impressed.

'I'm sorry, Kate,' she said. 'I'm afraid I felt too tired to argue. I've been feeling a bit under the weather just recently.'

She did look a big grey round the eyes and her blusher was brighter than usual.

'That's OK, Mrs Peterson,' I said, 'but d'you think it'd be all right if I dropped by later?'

'I should ring first, darling,' she said. 'Chas was muttering something about going off down to the ramps later, if he finished his work. He wants to try out his new board.'

37

This was desperate!

'Tell him I'll definitely be dropping in for a bit,' I said, 'and please can he wait to go out until afterwards? I really need to speak to him.'

'I'm sure that'll be fine,' said Mrs Charming. 'I'll see you later, Kate.'

As soon as lunch was over and Gran, who is always allowed to escape her nursing home on a Sunday, was safely nodding in an armchair, I pounced on Dad. He looked like he was settling down for a quick nap too.

'Will you give me a lift up to Chas's if I take Rover and walk him back?' I said. I know how to handle my dad. He walks Rover on Sundays because it's a busy day for Mum; she's started to do one of the church services each week because she's building up to going back to her work as a part-time vicar. Maternity leave doesn't last forever.

'Sounds like a good plan to me,' he said. 'If you make me a coffee first, I'll do it.'

Half an hour later, having rung to check that he hadn't gone out, I was at the door of Chas's den. Just as I'd suspected, he wasn't doing homework at all; he was playing on his computer. I crept up on him and clamped my hands round his neck.

'Die, traitor!' I hissed in his ear. 'Why weren't you at church? I wanted to speak to you.'

To my surprise, he was angry. 'You've just wrecked what I was doing!' he snapped. 'I'll have to start that level all over again!'

Looking back on it, this would have been a really good moment to pray. Spotted. It would kind of fit with asking someone why they weren't at *church*. So did I do it? No. You bet I didn't. Instead, I opened my big mouth – as usual.

'Ooh, my heart bleeds,' I said, nettled. 'Your mum said you were tired and had too much homework. It doesn't look that way to me!'

'So?' said Chas, rudely. 'Mind your own business if you don't like what you see!'

'Chas!' I said. 'Chas! It's me, Kate! Your friend! Why are you being so horrible?'

'Horrible? I'm not being horrible! You're the one who just wrecked my game and nearly gave me heart failure!'

'It was a joke, Chas! A surprise! What's happened to your sense of humour?'

'Maybe it's matured,' said Chas.

I turned my back. To my horror, my eyes had begun to prickle with tears. What had happened to my friend? He'd transformed from Mr Nice Guy to Mr Nasty almost overnight! With an effort, I pulled myself together.

'Look,' I said, forcing myself to sound light-hearted. 'Let's try that again, OK? From where I came in. Rewind.' I did a feeble impression of a tape rewinding and walked backwards to the door. Then I tapped on it and stepped into the room again.

'Hi Chas,' I said. 'It's me, Kate.'

'Hi Kate,' said Chas, his eyes glued to the screen again.

'Can I bring Rover in?' I said. 'I tied him up outside.'

'Yeah, OK.'

I unfastened Rover and he bounded into the den, rushing over to lick Chas's hand. Unlike me, he didn't get brushed aside. Chas actually let go of the mouse to fondle his head.

I sat down on the beaten-up sofa and waited. Rover came to join me and I made room beside me. I shouldn't have – even in a tatty old place like Chas's den, Rover ought to know his place and stay on the floor but I wanted his warm, friendly body next to me. You can always rely on Rover for a cheering doggy grin.

'Chas,' I said, after about five minutes, 'Chas, I want to talk to you. That's why I came. Didn't your Mum tell you?'

'Oh yeah, sorry,' he said, still not looking at me. 'I'm just finishing this level. You don't mind, do you?'

I suppose he had a point. In the past, we've spent hours in his den with one or both of us reading or playing on the computer. Today though, I thought it was obvious that I wanted to talk. He seemed to be being deliberately dense. My temper began to rise.

'Yes, I do mind actually,' I said. 'Why do you think I did all that "I'll come in again" stuff?'

Chas shrugged. 'Dunno really,' he said. He still wasn't listening to me properly.

I leaped across the space between us and shoved at the mouse wildly. It skidded off the desk and into mid-air.

'Kate!' exclaimed Chas. I'd got his full attention now. 'What on earth are you playing at? Who do you think you are, coming in here, telling me what to do?'

For a moment, I was speechless. 'Your friend,' I said, at last. 'I thought I was your *friend*. I thought you might *want* to talk to me!'

'Yeah, OK,' said Chas, 'but can't you wait just five minutes?'

'I've been waiting five minutes!' I shouted. 'I've been waiting since yesterday afternoon, if you really want to know! But first you were too busy being cool in front of your skater gang, then you were too busy to come to church and now you're too busy playing on the computer! Not so very long ago, you gave me a really hard time because I wasn't writing to you enough when you were at boarding school and now you won't even *speak* to me! What's the matter? Do I embarrass you, all of a sudden? Don't your new friends like you hanging out with "that vicar's kid"?'

Chas blushed and cleared his throat. So I was right. They'd had a go at him about me. They'd probably been having a go at him about going to church too.

'Well?' I said, impatiently. 'Is that it, then? No Kate, no church – because the skaters say so? No God either or d'you just keep quiet about him?'

If I'd stopped there, maybe things wouldn't have got as bad as they did. Looking back, that's what I should have done. But I'm always rushing in and saying the wrong thing. Today I did it big time.

'What are you?' I said. 'A complete wimp? I see how it is. Kate's all right when you haven't got anyone else – when you're lonely and a loser at boarding school then it's "Oh Kate! Where are you Kate? Why don't you write to me, Kate?"

You don't like it when Kate fancies another boy then! And when you run away because you can't hack it any longer then it's OK to run to the vicar and hope she sorts everything out – that's all fine. But now that you've suddenly joined the skateboard crew, then Kate's a bit of an embarrassment really. Kate and her Big Bum Mum – you'd rather have nothing to do with us any more! You'd rather we just kept out of your life! And as for church – well, forget it!'

Whenever Chas and I row, I'm the one who does the shouting. He goes cold and calm and mean. You can't clear the air with a good blast at each other like I do at home; if you could, maybe I wouldn't be sitting here pouring this all out now. Chas was scarlet with fury but all he did was pick up his mouse and turn back to his screen.

'If that's what you think, fine,' he said. 'See you around, Kate.'

'Chas!' I wailed. 'Is that it then? See you around? After all that grief you gave me at New Year? Chas, you were even jealous of Rover then!'

'Things change,' said Chas.

I didn't know what to say; I felt like my whole world had shifted into an alien space. I reached out to Rover for comfort and found him, tail wagging, jaws clamped on something that now resembled a gigantic piece of doggy chewing gum. He couldn't grin at me but thumped his tail in delight.

'Rover!' I shrieked. 'What on earth are you eating?'

There was a faint chocolately smell about the lump of goo but that was the only hint as to what he'd got hold of.

'Chas, I...'

But Chas had finally abandoned his game.

'He's got my skateboard wax!' he shouted. 'I only bought it yesterday! Help me, Kate!'

Instead, I laughed. Only a quick, surprised snort but I couldn't help it. Rover had mistaken Chas's attack on his jaw for love and promptly rolled over for his tummy to be tickled, kicking Chas in the face in the process.

'Skateboard wax?' I gasped. 'Then why on earth does it smell of chocolate?'

'It just does,' raged Chas. 'You can get cola and banana and everything. Now come and help me, can't you? He's your wretched dog! And don't laugh!'

'Well, let go of him then, you idiot,' I said. 'He thinks you want to play.'

Chas stood back, breathing heavily.

'Lie down, Rover,' I said. 'Now drop!'

I knew Rover couldn't drop the wax – it was well and truly stuck to his teeth – but at least he would open his mouth and I might be able to scoop some of it out. It'd be no use for skateboarding but now I was worried about the effect it might have on Rover's insides. He once ate a plastic bag and it nearly killed him.

Rover obligingly opened his mouth and panted; chunks of chewed brown goo were still stuck to his teeth and chocolate scented saliva dripped from his jaw.

'Yuk!' I said. 'I'm sorry, Chas, but I think you've seen the last of that wax.'

'Well, you can pay for it,' he said. 'It was brand new.'

I would, of course, have offered to pay but Chas jumping down my throat like that annoyed me all over again.

'Well, you should look after it better then,' I said. 'It must have just been lying around on the sofa for him to have got it.'

'You shouldn't have let him on the sofa.'

'You should have paid attention to me when I came in,' I said. 'Then it would never have happened.'

We glared at each other. Part of me wanted to reach out and grab him and beg him to forget the whole stupid episode, the other part was still smarting and furious and too upset to string any sensible words together.

'Oh, forget about the money,' said Chas, too quickly for me. 'Just go away and leave me alone.'

I took one last look at his back, rigid and unfriendly, as he picked up his mouse again. What was the point of trying again?

I clicked my fingers at Rover and he jumped off the sofa, leaving a trail of sticky brown saliva. I didn't care.

'Goodbye Chas,' I said and walked out of the den.

I cried on the way home. Well, wouldn't you? Partly, I cried because I was angry – when I think about it, I've spent a large part of the last two years worrying about my friendship with Chas. But mostly I cried because I was sad – I mean, I've also spent a large part of the last two years having a great time with him. It looks like I've just said goodbye to all that. I've seen it happen to other boys – the Kevin and Perry thing where they suddenly turn into grunting oiks overnight – but I'd never expected it with Chas. He gets moody – well, so do I – but this is more like he's had a complete brain transplant.

A couple of years back, when Mum fractured her skull, he was the one who got me started praying for her. Now here he is skiving church – OK, I know it's only been once – but maybe he's even giving up on God. I didn't realize how much that matters to me. I mean, if you grow up with a vicar for a mum, you tend to go with the flow. Church is just part of what you do, like other kids get dragged along to football matches or car boot sales. Gradually, I've got into praying and, though Mum and Dad do irritate me with their ability to quote the Bible come hell or high water (Question: what's that expression about then? I mean, neither hell nor high water sound like a good option to me!), I do think there's a lot of truth in what they say. But I still have really flaky moments when I wonder if I believe in God just because that's what I'm used to. And sometimes I think that praying is a complete waste of time. But it really upsets me to think Chas might not believe any of it any more. I guess I've thought of him as a kind of soulmate or (if you've ever read *Anne of Green Gables*) a kindred spirit. Maybe I've made a big mistake.

As I was trudging home, head down, hands in pockets, trying to pray (that's one really good thing about prayer – you can do it when there's nothing else you can possibly do, any place, any time), it began to rain.

Thank you, God, I thought, viciously. Thanks for nothing. Deep sigh. Just call me Wednesday.

* * *

When I got home, soaking wet and with a soggy dog to clean up, all I wanted was some nice, kind person to make me a lovely hot drink and give me a bit of sympathy. Instead, I found Belladonna in the kitchen with the twins.

'Your mother is lying down,' she announced. 'She feels exhausted. Your father has taken your grandmother back to her home. I said I would look after the twins for an hour as no one else was here.' She gave me an accusing glare. 'Where have you been, Kate? You look a mess.'

'I've been for a walk,' I growled. 'Isn't it obvious? And this is a free country, you know. I'm not the unpaid babysitter; I do have a life, believe it or not.'

'But you are not enjoying it,' said Belladonna, raising an eyebrow.

For a moment, I thought I detected an atom of sympathy. Then I thought the better of it – this was Belladonna talking, wasn't it? I stomped off upstairs and started running a bath. Still no mango bubble bath, of course – and that set me off crying, all over again. That bubble bath might have been my last present from Chas and I'd only used it a couple of times. I sat down on the loo and had a good howl. No one could hear me because the taps were on.

I had just stepped out of the bath, feeling slightly more human, when I heard a shriek from the sitting room that sent me hurtling down the stairs, hair dripping and bathrobe clutched hurriedly around me.

The stench as I opened the door made me gag. Paraffin

wax and chocolate with a strong hint of dog. The scene was worse. Shivering by the gas fire, where I had left him to dry out, was Rover, looking utterly woebegone. Standing with her hand pressed to her mouth and Hayley on her hip was Belladonna, her face vaguely green. Split seconds away from a greasy brown mound by the door, crawled Comet.

I swooped and picked her up with one arm, hauled Rover to his feet with the other and then dragged him through the kitchen and out of the back door where he promptly produced another nasty heap on the grass.

'Good boy,' I said and left him, poor thing, standing in the rain gazing mournfully after me.

Belladonna was throwing up in spectacular fashion in the sink, Hayley was screaming because she'd just been dumped in her playpen and Comet, startled at being rushed out into the pouring rain, promptly joined in. Togetherness. Wonderful. I love it.

Mum staggered in, looking tousled and exhausted, just as Ben arrived at the back door with his girlfriend, Suzie.

'Why's Rover...?' he started and then, 'Blimey... is anyone *not* crying?'

I glanced round. The babies were still sobbing, Belladonna had stopped being sick but had started to weep and BGM, looking totally unlike the mum I knew, was leaning against the doorframe, her shoulders shuddering.

'My head,' she moaned. 'It feels like it's going to split open.'

'*I'm* not crying,' I snapped. 'And if you want to know why

Rover's outside, go and look in the sitting room.'

Ben picked up Hayley, held her close and blew a raspberry at her. 'Go to bed, Mum,' he said. 'Dad'll be back soon.'

Mum didn't argue. I passed Comet to Ben; we're both pretty adept at juggling babies but I knew he'd make them laugh and I just wasn't in the mood.

'I guess I get to clear up the pooch poop,' I said, bitterly. 'Excuse me while I slip into something more comfortable.'

Outside, Rover was howling miserably. All we needed was a complaint from the neighbours and I'm sure every sound was like a bullet through Mum's head. I pulled on my oldest jeans and sweatshirt as fast as I could and then set to in the sitting room. Speed was vital anyway; if I wasn't quick, I'd be following Belle's example. Thank goodness the torrential rain was dealing with the pile in the garden! It's lucky that the carpet is an indeterminate beige colour. We all hate it (it came with the house) and Mum has tried to brighten it up with a Fair Trade rug but I was grateful for it this afternoon. Imagine getting recycled chocolate-scented skateboard wax off something cream and luxurious!

As soon as I'd finished, I checked on Rover who had taken refuge under a bush.

'I think he's finished,' said Ben. 'What on earth has he eaten?'

I explained.

'Crikey!' said Ben. 'I bet Chas wasn't very happy.'

'Just don't talk to me about Chas!' I spat. '*I'm* not very happy, if you really want to know.'

'Sorry I spoke,' said Ben.

I led Rover back into the kitchen and rubbed him down. He licked my face gratefully which almost made me cry again. Poor old thing! He must be feeling rotten and I'd made him stand out in the rain. But what else could I do?

The kettle was humming, the babies were happily jiggling the various toys strapped to the side of the playpen and Ben was scrubbing out the sink with disinfectant. As little brothers go, I thought, he's not all that bad.

The next moment, I changed my mind. Ben left the sink, made a pot of tea and poured out a mugful. Then he reached for the sugar pot.

'I don't take sugar,' I said, puzzled.

'Oh, this is if for Belle,' Ben said. 'She's gone to lie down – she was feeling really ill. There's more in the pot.'

He left with the mug. I was too staggered for words. I get to clean up the poo, I get to clean up the dog and Belle gets the tea and the sympathy! I'm sure the Bible has something to say about that – something about being partial to the wicked and depriving the innocent of justice. I think it's one of the Proverbs. I rather like them. Here's one I could particularly apply to Belladonna:

'Beauty in a woman without good judgment is like a gold ring in a pig's snout.'

Or in other words:

'What use are bella bella boobs if you're sick at the sight of pooch poop?'

Oops, I suspect that's vitriol again. Naughty, naughty, Kate!

Slapped wrist! There's another verse, one of Mum's all-time favourites about 'humbly considering others better than yourself'. I definitely need to work on it!

4

My Mum and
Mrs Charming Peterson

It didn't take my friend Vicky long to notice that something
was wrong between Chas and me.

'OK, what have you done to Chas this time?' she said,
pouncing on me at breaktime.

'Me?' I said, outraged. 'Why d'you think it's me? It's him
that's gone stomping off to join his skateboard mates and
didn't even speak to me in tutor period!'

'OK, chill will you?' said Vicky. 'I just know that whatever
he's done to upset you, you probably opened your big mouth
and made it one hundred times worse!'

'Cheek!' I gasped.

'Don't argue,' said Vicky. 'You know I'm right.'

I did – only too well.

Vicky rolled her eyes. 'Honestly,' she said. 'You two! What
are you like?'

'Dunno really,' I said. 'Best friends one minute, worst

enemies the next. I never seem to get it right.'

'The trouble is,' said Vicky, 'that whenever you're upset with each other, he says nothing but you shout at him. It all goes inside with him but it all comes out with you.'

'That's why I write my journal,' I said.

'I know,' said Vicky. 'Just as well. Goodness knows what you'd say if you didn't. But Chas isn't that type. It looks like there's nothing wrong but really it's all festering away inside.'

'Are you training to be a shrink or something?' I said.

'I think I'd be really good at it,' said Vicky. 'I get enough practice with you and Chas forever falling out!'

'D'you think something's upset him then?' I asked.

'You mean, apart from you?'

'Yes… I mean, he started leaving me out of things before I yelled at him yesterday. That's *why* I yelled at him.'

'I don't know,' said Vicky. 'Teenage boys are all weird, if you ask me. I mean, look at them. Either they don't have a clue what to wear and don't care or they're forever poncing about in front of the mirror, imagining that if they spray themselves with Lynx they'll smell better. And then there are the obsessions.'

'Obsessions?'

'Oh yeah,' said Vicky. 'They've all got one. There's the sad, geeky sort that get into trainspotting or Warhammer, or the football sort that can't do anything except swear and hog the TV, or the rock band sort that get surgically attached to their guitars. They're all bonkers – I mean, do you see *girls* doing air guitar?'

'Oh,' I said. 'So what sort's Chas?'

'Skateboarding sort, obviously. Not unlike the football sort except that they try to break their necks more.'

'So what do I do? Just hang on and wait for him to break his neck?'

'Most of them seem to grow out of it,' said Vicky. 'It's just a phase. I mean, once they get a job, they haven't time to be quite so obsessed.'

'I don't know,' I said. 'The football sort never seem to get over it!'

'Well, don't marry one of them then,' said Vicky. 'Anyway, Chas is the skateboarding sort. You don't see many middle-aged skateboarders.'

'They've probably all had their necks broken,' I said glumly. 'And anyway, I don't want to wait till Chas is middle-aged; I want my friend back now!'

Vicky shrugged. 'Well, it won't help nagging him about it. You've just got to be patient. At least he's not obsessed with girls. You'd hate that even worse.'

'I don't know,' I said, biting my nails. 'I think there's more to this than skateboarding. I mean, it's not like he seems really happy. You'd think that if skateboarding was such a big thing for him, he'd at least look like he's enjoying it.'

'It's all image,' said Vicky. 'You have to look cool and mean. And anyway, maybe he isn't much good at it yet. That might be depressing him.'

'Then why do it, if he's no good?'

'Why do it anyway? Why jump down flights of steps on a bit

of wood with wheels when you could run down on two legs? How am I supposed to know? Like I said, boys are just weird.'

I wasn't satisfied.

'The thing is,' I said, 'I don't think his mum and dad have been getting on too well. They really disagreed about sending him away to school. Chas said his dad'll do anything for a quiet life but he really wasn't happy about it at all. He thought they should send Chas back. He was furious about all the wasted money and thought Mrs C was being all namby-pamby with Chas.'

'Well, have they been rowing about it?' asked Vicky. 'It's quite a while ago now.'

'Not as far as I know. Chas hasn't said much. They're the sort of people who keep things quiet – well, his dad is, anyway.'

'Just like Chas, then,' said Vicky.

'Yes, I suppose so... it's just... well, I saw Chas's mum yesterday and she didn't look herself at all. Kind of tired and feeble looking.'

'Maybe it's the menopause,' said Vicky. 'Or a bad headache. Or both. Honestly, Kate, you do get your knickers in a twist about things. Just chill, will you? Chas is being a normal teenage boy. It's no fun but it's the way he's going to be for a while. Live with it, OK?'

I pulled a face. 'I suppose you're right,' I said. But I wasn't happy. It nagged at me all day. I just couldn't quite believe that Chas's behaviour was normal – for him, at any rate. He's never been normal. When I first got to know him he was into reading the *Little House on the Prairie* books! Chas? A normal teenage boy? No way.

I thought I might have a word with Mum about it. She's always got on well with Chas and I knew she was surprised by his rudeness on Saturday. But when I got home, there was another shock waiting for me.

Parked outside the house was Mrs Charming Peterson's car. I strolled into the house, expecting to find Mum and Mrs C putting the world to rights over a cup of tea in the kitchen. Instead, I found Belladonna scrubbing potatoes, and the babies in their playpen.

'Where's Mum?' I asked.

'In the sitting room,' said Belladonna, 'but...'

I should have waited. I shouldn't have gone bounding in. But I was impatient to see Mum and never imagined the scene that met my eyes.

Mrs Immaculate Charming Peterson was sitting on the sofa, her make-up in ruins, sobbing her heart out. Mum had her arm round her and was making soothing noises like she does to the babies. I didn't need her silent glare to send me scuttling back out of the room again, praying that Mrs C hadn't noticed my intrusion.

I shot back into the kitchen, ignoring Rover's plaintive whines (he'd been banished to his bed in the hall).

Belladonna looked at me over her shoulder.

'You should have listened to me,' she said. 'Mrs Peterson has a problem.'

'I know. I'm sorry,' I said, automatically.

Belladonna raised her eyebrows. She isn't used to me being civil to her.

'Is it something very bad?' she asked. 'You look... what is the expression? Like you have seen a ghost?'

'I don't know, I didn't hear,' I said. 'But I've never seen Mrs Peterson cry before – and she was in floods.'

'In floods?'

'Crying a lot. You know, like a flood. Loads of tears.'

'You like this woman?' asked Belladonna. 'She is not only your mother's friend?'

'Yes. Yes, I do,' I said, surprising myself. Mrs Peterson is a gushy, fussy woman who frequently drives me round the bend but she is also one of the kindest people I have ever met. I'd never really acknowledged that before. And she's the sort you expect to carry on coping whatever the crisis. I was shocked rigid to see her crumple.

Belladonna put down the potato peeler.

'I will make you some tea, Kate,' she said. 'You are very pale.'

This unexpected kindness from Belle nearly finished me off. I gulped hard and swallowed my tears. I still didn't trust her. She was smiling kindly now but so do crocodiles. I wasn't going to cry in front of her.

'Thank you,' I croaked. 'Thanks very much.'

Ben had dawdled home the long way round via Suzie's. When he arrived I'd finished the tea and the chocolate biscuit that

Belladonna had found and was feeling a little better.

'Ben,' I said, 'I have to talk to you.'

'What, right now?' said Ben. 'Let me put my bag down, can't you?' He turned to the twins, who were crowing to be picked up. They really love their big brother. He crouched beside the playpen and pulled faces at them through the bars, making them chortle with delight.

'Let's go in the sitting room,' he said. 'Then we can take these two with us.'

'We can't,' I said. 'That's what I've got to talk to you about. Come up to my room.'

'You've been eating chocolate biscuits,' he said, spotting the crumbs on my plate. 'Where are they?'

'I am sorry, Ben, it was the last one,' said Belladonna. 'I gave it to Kate because she was upset.'

'You gave the last chocolate biscuit to Kate?' gasped Ben. 'How could you, Belle? You know that I'll die without chocolate!'

Belladonna prodded him in the tummy.

'Less chocolate would be good for you, young man,' she said with a roguish grin, making Ben blush.

'Come on, Ben,' I said coldly. 'Let's go upstairs. Perhaps Belle would like to make you some tea when we've finished talking, seeing as she's so concerned about your welfare?'

Ben shrugged and followed me out of the door.

'Miaow!' he said and clawed at the air.

'Well, honestly,' I said. 'Flirting with you like that! It's obscene! You're only thirteen.'

'Oh take a chill pill, Kate,' said Ben. 'You're always so serious. It's not surprising Chas is getting fed up with you.'

'Is that what he's said?' I snapped, stock-still on the stairs.

'No, but it's obvious, isn't it? That's why he's hanging out with that skateboarding crew.'

I felt like he'd thrust a cold knife into my chest. Seriously. This horrible, sick, chilly feeling was spreading out from my heart. Was that it, then? Was he bored with me? Then I remembered Mrs Charming, sobbing downstairs on the sofa.

'There's more to it than that,' I said. 'We need to talk.'

'Talk all you like,' shrugged Ben. 'It won't change anything. Chas is getting bored with you. Get used to it.'

I pushed Ben into my bedroom.

'I don't believe you,' I said. 'He can be interested in skateboarding without it meaning he's bored with me!'

Ben shrugged. 'I don't know,' he said. 'I'd be bored with you. Who wants to hang around with a girl and not snog her?'

For a moment, I was speechless. 'Ben, you are so crude,' I said, at last. 'Is that how you see Suzie? Just someone to snog?'

'No, stupid! I've told you before. Suzie's my best friend *and* I like snogging her. But it'd drive me mad to be hanging round with a girl and *not* snogging her. Where would be the fun in that?'

Again, I was struggling for words. 'Don't you *talk* to her at all?' I said.

'Talk? Of course I talk – well, Suzie could talk for England so I don't get much of a look in. But talking gets boring after a while.'

'Well, don't you like doing things together? Walking the dog? Going to the cinema?'

''Course I do – but there's more to life than that. That's why I do Scouts and rollerblading and stuff. Stuff with the lads. It's perfect. Suzie's for chatting and snogging. The lads are for everything else. The trouble with you, Kate, is that all you do is chat. Chas needs to break out a bit, that's all.'

I looked at Ben dubiously. He had shocked me to the core but I could see his point. Chas has always been a bit of a loner and I've assumed he's happy with that – but maybe he isn't. Maybe he's finally found the friends he's been looking for. I'm OK but I'm not enough. But Ben's idea that girls are for chatting and snogging is outrageous. I couldn't let him get away with that.

'Does Suzie know what you think of her?' I demanded.

'Dunno really,' said Ben. 'She doesn't get all steamed up about things like you do. You should relax, Kate. Don't get your knickers in a twist. Move on. Make some new friends. If Chas really likes you, he'll still be there. If he doesn't, you might as well forget him anyway.'

Sometimes I hate Ben. It's the way he seems to have everything sussed; the way he just strolls through life as if he hasn't a care in the world. He only gets stressed about the big things, like Mum nearly dying in that bike accident a couple of years ago. It's unreasonable for someone of thirteen to be quite so together, especially when I'm such a heaving mass of stress and confusion.

'Look, this isn't what I want to talk about,' I said. 'You make it all sound so simple – but I don't think it's as straightforward as that. Downstairs in the lounge, Mrs Charming Peterson is crying all over Mum. Seriously. She's weeping buckets.'

It was Ben's turn to look stunned. 'Mrs Peterson?' he said. 'Are you sure?'

'Of course I'm sure. I went barging in by mistake. She looked a complete wreck.'

'Maybe someone's died,' suggested Ben. 'Her mother?'

'What, that old battleaxe?' I said. I'd only met Mrs C's mother once but she didn't look like the type to die early. (Question: why do the most difficult people always seem to stay alive the longest? Because they're so determined to be difficult?)

'Well, it must be something really bad,' said Ben. 'I can't imagine Mrs Peterson *crying!* '

'No, neither can I, but she was. The thing is, I'm wondering if it's to do with her and Mr Peterson not getting on.'

'What?' said Ben. 'Why on earth do you think that?'

'Because they really disagreed about all that boarding school business with Chas.'

'Don't be silly, Kate,' said Ben. 'People don't get divorced over things like that!'

'I bet they do,' I said, 'but the other thing is, it doesn't seem to me that they've *ever* got on very well. I mean, they hardly seem to talk to one another – not like Mum and Dad.'

'There you go again! Talking, talking! What's the big deal with talking?' protested Ben. 'Mr Peterson is a quiet sort of chap who likes pigs. There probably isn't much to talk about!'

'But they're married, Ben! They *must* talk to each other!'

'Don't see why. You just expect everyone to be like you – and they're not. You're imagining things, Kate. You *want* Chas to be all screwed up about something so you're inventing it!'

'I didn't invent Mrs Charming crying!'

'OK, so there's something wrong with Mrs C – but it doesn't mean she's about to get a divorce! Chas is fine – he just wants to live a little!'

At that moment, there was a tap on my door. It was Mum. I blushed.

'Sorry, Mum,' I said. 'Barging in like that. I wanted to talk to you and I didn't wait to hear what Belle was saying. Did Mrs Peterson notice?'

'No, I think she was too upset,' said Mum. 'I suppose you've told Ben?'

I blushed even more. Thinking about it now, I realized I should have kept quiet. Mrs C wouldn't want everyone knowing her business.

'Sorry, Mum,' I said again.

'It's not OK but I forgive you anyway,' she said. 'Just try to think before you open that big mouth of yours, Kate.'

'Yes, Mum. Sorry, Mum.' Only I knew how much I wished I could learn to do as she said!

'Anyway, I want you both to keep quiet about it,' Mum continued. 'Mrs Peterson doesn't want anyone else to know what's wrong so I'm afraid you'll just have to quell your curiosity.'

Ben and I both nodded sensibly but of course I was dying to know what was going on.

'So you're quite clear about that, both of you?' said Mum. 'Not a word to anyone, all right?'

Again, we agreed and Mum left.

'You see?' I said immediately. 'It's a secret! Maybe Mr Peterson's had an affair or something!'

'In your dreams!' retorted Ben. 'Mr Peterson? He's not the type!'

'Everyone always thinks that until it happens,' I said. 'Maybe Chas suspects something and that's why he's gone all grumpy.'

'Yeah, that really makes sense,' said Ben. 'My parents are splitting up… mmm… I think I'll get into skateboarding. Yeah right, Kate.'

'Don't you understand, Ben?' I insisted. 'If things are tense at home, then skateboarding would be ideal! You can get out of the way for hours on end!'

'Chas can do that anyway – he's got a den,' Ben reminded me.

'Oh, I don't care what you say,' I said. 'There's obviously something wrong – and it's making Chas go peculiar, that's all.'

'Well, if that's what you want to believe…' said Ben. 'But if I were you, I'd try snogging him.'

I threw a cushion at him. 'Go away,' I said. 'You're obsessed. Vicky's right. Teenage boys are just bonkers.'

'So are teenage girls,' said Ben. 'Especially you.'

Then he shot out of the door before I could get my hands on him and do any serious damage.

I sat down at my computer and started to type.

The next moment, Ben was back.

'Mum's been crying too, you know,' he said. 'Just thought you might want to know, Sherlock Holmes.'

'Well, she might cry if her friend's marriage is breaking up,' I said.

'What, Mum?' scoffed Ben. 'She's pretty tough, you know. No, it's got to be something worse than that. Someone's died, I bet you.'

'Why would that be a secret?' I demanded. 'Go away, Ben. I want to get on with my journal. But I bet I'm right. You just wait and see.'

'Huh,' said Ben. 'A fiver on it?'

I don't normally join in Ben's bets but this time, I felt I had something to prove. My honour was at stake.

'Done,' I said. 'But make it a tenner, OK?'

'You'll regret that,' said Ben, and left.

5

My Mum and Gran

I didn't so much regret the bet as forget about it completely.
Today, something terrible happened that put Mrs Charming
Peterson right out of my mind.

Our gran has been getting increasingly frail for a couple of
years. For as long as I remember, she's been distinctly dotty.
She's very old, as grannies go. She didn't have Dad till she was
in her late thirties which was very unusual in those days and
then Mum and Dad were slow having Ben and me too. So I
never knew Gran at her best. A while back she had pneumonia
and since then she's been particularly fragile and especially
potty. Even so, she's had her uses. The twins think she's
hilarious and it was she who convinced Mum that Rover was
dying when he swallowed that plastic bag.

Dad was just setting off for work and the rest of us were
shovelling down breakfast when the phone call came. We
could tell from his face and the clipped way he was speaking
that it was something serious.

'It's Mother,' he said. 'She collapsed having breakfast. Heart attack. If I go straight to the hospital, I might get there in time. Jo, I...'

'Don't worry, just go, darling,' said Mum. 'I'll get this lot sorted out and then see if I can get down there too.'

Dad hesitated. 'What will I need?' he asked. 'I can't think straight.'

'Nothing except your wallet and your keys,' said Mum. 'Now go!'

Dad didn't wait even to drop his usual kiss on Mum's cheek. He just slurped the rest of his coffee and ran.

'Kate, can you ring the salon and leave a message that Dad won't be in?' said Mum. 'Tell them what's happened and ask them to cancel his clients for the next few days.'

I stood up, limp-legged and shaky, but I didn't want to ring. I didn't want to face what was happening. I had to though; Mum was busy with the babies and Belladonna hadn't come down yet.

'Mum, what might Dad not get there in time for?' asked Ben, in a tremulous voice. 'Not...?'

'Yes, love, I'm afraid so,' said Mum. 'It's obviously very serious. He's hoping to be in time to say goodbye.'

Mum still sent us to school.

'Where there's life, there's hope,' she said but I think she just wanted us out of the way. I could see why. She had enough on her plate with the babies and a possible funeral to organize without us hanging around. Not that we're useless –

we can be very helpful when we have to be – but I didn't feel like being helpful just then. I felt like a zombie. I couldn't concentrate on anything. I didn't feel like crying; after all, Gran wasn't dead yet – I just felt weird – numb and disembodied. I told Vicky, of course. I wanted to tell Chas. He knows Gran well and only a couple of months back, I'd have gone rushing to him – but, as per usual, he was hanging around with his skateboarding mates. Worse, these two girls called Lisa and Donna were there too. Lisa's always fancied Chas and often tries to cause trouble between us. I couldn't bear the thought of being snubbed by him in front of her.

'Kate, why on earth have you come to school?' said Vicky. 'You should have stayed at home!'

'Mum thought it might take our minds off it, I think. Well, actually, I don't think she was thinking straight at all – she just wanted to get us out of the way.'

'Oh well,' said Vicky. 'I suppose you'd only be hanging around worrying at home. Come on – jolly old Maths first.'

I couldn't concentrate on Maths, of course, even though it's a subject I really like. All I could think about was Gran. Fortunately, our teacher, Mr Allen, is one of the best.

'What's up, Kate?' he asked, stopping by my desk. 'It's not like you to look so vacant.'

He was teasing but concerned. Suddenly, I couldn't speak, I felt so choked.

'It's her Gran,' said Vicky quietly. 'They think she's dying.'

'Aah,' said Mr Allen. 'Not easy to focus on Maths then.

Would you like to go out, Kate?'

I shook my head. 'I'd rather stay,' I croaked. 'But I might not get very much done.'

'No problem,' said Mr Allen. 'Let me know if you change your mind.'

I survived Maths in a blur but by the end of break, I realized I'd had enough. Not every teacher would be so understanding and Vicky and I are in different sets for French so I wouldn't have her support. The sight of her back disappearing into the crowd finished me off. I got out my mobile.

Belle answered. 'Ah… Kate,' she said. 'Ermm… I will fetch your mother.'

Her hesitation told me all I needed to know.

'She's dead, isn't she?' I blurted when Mum came to the phone. I heard her intake of breath. Was she wondering whether to lie, to get me through the school day?

'Yes, Kate, she is. It was shortly after you left for school. Phil got there in time. He says she was very peaceful.' There was a pause. 'Would you like to come home, love?'

'Yes… no… I don't know.' I had run out of words. Even though I'd expected it, the news had me reeling.

'Kate? Kate? Are you still there?' Mum's voice was anxious.

'Er… yes… look, I'll ring you if I want to come home,' I said. My brain felt like it had bobbed off to a place disconnected from my body, but I knew that the last thing Mum needed was to drive up to school to get me.

I stood there, in the middle of the corridor, rooted to the

spot. People were shoving into me and banging me with their bags but I couldn't move. I had wanted to know but the news had paralysed me.

A boy stopped and spoke to me.

'Kate?' he said. 'Kate? Are you all right? You look really weird.'

It was Greg, gorgeous or grotty, depending on your point of view. His words jolted my brain back into action. I suddenly remembered how kind he had been when Gran was taken poorly a few months ago.

'I just phoned home,' I said. 'My gran just died.'

I looked up and registered the shock on Greg's face. 'Oh Kate,' he said. 'I'm so sorry. Was it very sudden?'

I nodded dumbly and the next moment was bawling. Greg was heroic. He wrapped his arm round me and shoved his way through the crowds of kids until he got me to Reception, which is where you go whether you've lost your lunch money or you've broken your leg.

'Her gran's just died,' he said, startling the receptionist. 'I'm going to find her brother. My mum or dad will give them a lift home if you ring them.'

At that moment, Chas sauntered by with a bunch of his mates. He saw me, I'm sure he did. Maybe he saw that Greg's hand was still resting on my shoulder, I don't know. It's still no excuse. He didn't stop to see what was wrong; he just carried on walking.

* * *

If anyone close to you has ever died, you'll know what it's like. People might think that you all spend hours sobbing your hearts out. Instead, there's simply masses to do. Registering the death, contacting the undertakers, planning the service, ordering flowers, answering the phone – it goes on and on. Especially answering the phone. Right now, it feels like the whole town knows either Mum or Dad and wants to express their sympathy. And I'm amazed by how many friends Gran still has who want to come to the funeral. Ben and I didn't feel like going to school the day after Gran died and it's just as well we didn't, we were so busy being polite. By the afternoon, we had a stream of callers to deal with. It was really odd: part of me was in this numb haze, unable to cry and feeling like I was special in some strange way; the other part was zinging with this huge adrenalin buzz like we were getting ready for a wedding or something.

Ben is crying a lot. He keeps going off to his room for breaks from the busyness or taking Rover out for yet another ten-minute run. The dog, at least, is blissfully happy. Ben always re-appears looking tear-stained and blotchy. Anybody who calls is overwhelmingly sympathetic and sets him off all over again.

I can't cry. I'm starting to wonder if there's something wrong with me. Belladonna keeps looking at me oddly. She probably thinks I'm as hard as nails. I'm beginning to think so myself.

Belladonna has got increasingly ratty; her workload seems to have doubled overnight.

'We'll pay you extra,' Dad assured her. 'I'm really sorry about this but we don't have any relatives who can come and help.'

I've always been rather glad of that – we've been spared an awful lot of boring visits, even if we don't get many Christmas presents and Easter eggs – but I can see why a helpful relative might be useful at a time like this. Mrs Charming Peterson has often helped us out in a crisis but she hasn't volunteered and I don't think I'd better suggest that we contact her.

I'd assumed Mum would lead the funeral service but she doesn't want to. She says she's too emotionally involved and might break down in the middle of it. That's meant more hassle as a different vicar had to be found who is free at a suitable time. He had to visit us to discuss how we wanted the service to go and Ben disgraced us all by having a tantrum over the hymns.

'Whatever else we have, we're not having "Abide with me",' said Dad. 'It's so hackneyed and has such a mournful tune.'

I drew in my breath. If I didn't miss my guess, he'd just lit the blue touchpaper. I was right.

'Gran loved it,' said Ben. 'And so do I. You have to have it. It's traditional, anyway.'

I knew only too well Ben's feelings about 'Abide with me'. The summer before last, he made me stand at the grave of his cat, Fergus, and sing it. I was caught in the act by Chas, on his first ever visit to our house. My cheeks blazed at the memory.

'Oh, shut up, Ben!' I snapped. 'Dad should choose. Gran was his mum, wasn't she?'

'Then why I are *we* sitting here?' demanded Ben. 'I thought we were *all* planning this service.'

The vicar tried to smooth things over. 'I was hoping you and Kate might want to read some words about your gran – or say a prayer or something. I like to involve children in funerals.'

I winced at Ben and me being called 'children' in that patronizing way but could see he was trying to be helpful. Ben was beyond seeing anything.

'Gran would want "Abide with me",' he insisted. 'She told me she liked it when Fergus died and Kate was all stressy about singing it.'

'Now don't drag that up, Ben,' said Mum. 'Kate sang it then but your dad doesn't want it now.'

'Well, *I* want it!' Ben shouted. 'And Gran would have wanted it! And if we don't have it, I won't come, so there!' And with that, he burst into tears – again.

Mum, Dad and the vicar were all sympathy, of course. I was just irritated.

'Kate, will you take him out and make him a cup of tea, darling?' Mum said. 'He's obviously getting overwrought about all this.'

I glowered at Mum. Overwrought, indeed! He was behaving like a spoilt brat. I grabbed him by the arm, harder than I should have done, and led him to the kitchen.

'Pull yourself together!' I told him. 'You're being pathetic. And make your own tea. Isn't there enough to do without you behaving like a baby?'

Ben didn't argue but slumped down at the table and snuffled into his sleeve.

Belladonna was keeping the real babies occupied with a packet of breadsticks. She gave me a withering look.

'*I'll* make you some tea, Ben,' she said. 'And I'm sure we've still got some chocolate biscuits.'

I shot out of the kitchen and slammed the door. Better that than slapping her smug, self-righteous face.

When I got back to the sitting room, they'd made their decision. 'Abide with me' would be sung by the choir, while people were gathering for the funeral. Typical! Ben's not being half as helpful as me, but he still gets his own way! Maybe I should cry and stamp my feet a bit. I wish I could; I feel like there's this great ticking bomb of horribleness inside me, just waiting to explode, but I can't do anything about it. Worse even than Wednesday.

Today, the bomb exploded. It was the day of the funeral. It was planned for two in the afternoon. If you ever have to plan a funeral, take my advice, have it first thing in the morning. If people have to set off at the crack of dawn, tough! At least you'll be spared all the hanging around not knowing what to do with yourself. BGM (and she was Big Glum Mum big time today) decided to tackle the job she'd been putting off and which no one else could face. It was unpacking the little bag of personal belongings that had been sent home from the hospital. There were only a few items but the bag had been sitting in the hall for several days. I'd been tempted to throw it in the bin – I mean, there was hardly likely to be anything worth keeping – but didn't think I could face confessing when the bag was finally missed.

I was the one who heard Mum crying in her bedroom, crying as if her heart would break. She, like me, had been keeping a stiff upper lip remarkably well. The men had crumpled but we women had kept the ship on course. I couldn't fetch Dad; he and Ben had gone down to the church hall to set up tables for the ladies from the Mothers' Union who were helping us with the funeral tea. I tiptoed into the room. Mum was kneeling at the bed, sobbing into a nightie of Gran's.

The numb, disembodied feeling came over me again. It was as if I was watching myself in a movie, as I knelt down next to her and put my arm around her shoulders. BGM turned and wrapped her arms round my neck, crying onto my shoulder.

'Oh Kate,' she wept. 'It's the smell. It just hit me as I opened the bag. Rose water and Nivea cream. It was as if she'd just walked into the room. I know she wasn't an easy woman – we didn't always get on – but I was very fond of her. I know she's in a better place now… I really do believe that… and I know I ought to be happy for her. But Kate, I'll miss her so much!'

And she started crying, all over again. I hugged her hard, realizing with a shock, that Mum had memories of Gran that went back to a time before her dotty old age. Even at her pottiest, Gran had been inclined to be critical of Mum. No, she couldn't have been the easiest person to have as a mother-in-law. Yet Mum was crying like a fountain, while I still felt as numb and chilly as a block of stone. I wondered if I was ever going to feel anything again. I couldn't even feel sad when I thought of Chas abandoning me in favour of the skateboard posse.

It was the flowers that did it. We had announced that there would be family flowers only and donations in lieu of flowers would be split between the Alzheimer's Society and Gran's favourite charity, The Leprosy Mission.

At about midday, the doorbell rang. I hurried to open it, Comet clutched to my hip.

A lady stood on the step with a monstrous floral cross in her arms.

'Flowers for Lofthouse,' she said.

I looked at the thing she was holding. I'd seen such horrors before in the church graveyard. They're made of that weird Oasis stuff, I think, and then hundreds of flower heads are stuck into them like a kind of giant pincushion. Vandalism, I've always thought. The wilful destruction of perfectly good flowers.

'I think there must be a mistake,' I said. 'We can't have ordered that.'

The woman looked at the label.

'Definitely Lofthouse,' she said. 'And I remember your Mum ordering it. She's the Reverend, isn't she? Very particular about the colours, she was.'

'Mum!' I hollered. 'Mum! Come here!'

I must have sounded like I'd amputated my hand or something. Mum came hurtling out of the kitchen, clutching Hayley.

'Kate? What on earth have you done?' she demanded.

'It's what you've done!' I spat at her. 'How could you order that awful thing?' Then I dumped Comet on the carpet where she promptly began to yell and ran for my room, my chest heaving as if Alien was about to burst out of it. I threw myself on my bed and all my pent-up grief came bursting out so hard that I was almost sick.

Mum pounded after me. Dimly, I could hear the twins bellowing in the hall.

'Kate!' Mum cried. 'Kate, your gran would have wanted one! She thought they were great. "No nasty cellophane and messy stems," she used to say. "They last for days and look very neat and tidy on the graves." That's why we chose one; I didn't think you'd mind.'

I struggled to sit up, choking on snot and tears.

'But I do mind!' I wailed. 'I want something special from me – not some horrible shared thing that I hate!'

Mum went to put her arms round me but I pushed her away.

'Don't touch me!' I yelled. 'Just leave me alone!'

She did. There was nothing she could have done; I was beside myself and I cried and cried until I was exhausted.

About an hour later, there was a tap on the door. It was Dad. He had brought me a couple of boiled eggs, some tea and toast.

'Kate,' he said, sitting down on my bed. 'You need to have something to eat.'

I nodded, taking the tray from him. I was ravenous now.

'Darling, if you'd rather not come to the funeral, that's fine,' he said.

'No, I want to come,' I said. Tears began to fill my eyes again. 'I just hate those flowers.'

'How would it be if you picked some from the garden?' he said. 'There are a few that aren't bad. Maybe you could make a little posy of your own.'

I managed a weak smile. 'A little bunch of dandelions?' I suggested. Gardening is not one of my family's strong points.

'I think we could manage something better than that,' he said. 'There's some nice pink stuff in bloom and lots of foliage.'

I nodded. It would be better than nothing. I knew I had some pretty ribbon in my craft basket.

'OK,' I said. 'So long as you don't mind.'

'Of course not,' said Dad. 'Just don't use cellophane or leave any messy stems.'

I gripped his hand and swallowed hard. He didn't need me bursting into tears all over again.

'I'm so proud of you, Kate,' he said. 'You've been so strong and brave over the last few days and such a help. We couldn't have managed without you.'

'I thought there was something wrong with me,' I said. 'I felt so weird. I couldn't cry – there was this big blockage inside me.'

'D'you feel a bit better now?' he asked.

I grimaced. 'Not really,' I said. 'Just a different kind of awful. It feels more normal, though.'

'I'm glad we got the horrid flowers then,' he said. ' "A different kind of awful" sounds like progress. I know exactly what you mean.'

He left me to eat my lunch. Then I slipped out to the garden and found what I could to make a posy. Gran would have understood, I'm sure. She knew what it was like to have strong feelings about things, however bonkers everyone else thinks you are.

6

My Mum and the Awful Au Pair - Again!

As funerals go, Gran's went well. That's what everyone said, anyway. I don't have much experience. It was lovely spring weather which helped. Some people like rain for a funeral – it suits the mood – but Gran was always so feisty and forthright that a brisk breeze and bright sunlight seemed very fitting. We sang her favourite songs and hymns; it seemed a shame that she wasn't there to join in, except in spirit perhaps, but we belted them out just the same. (Question: do some people go to church because they're good at singing or are they good at singing because they go to church?)

Loads of people came. I was staggered. Gran had been Headmistress of a junior school and a surprising number of her old pupils turned up. Then there were people from church, people from her old Bridge Club, people from CND (that was a surprise – apparently she'd been one of the women who protested about nuclear missiles being sited at Greenham Common) and people from a charity for battered women. It was eye-opening. I lost count of the number of people who told me what a clever or interesting or dynamic woman she had been. It gave me pause for thought, I can tell you. I remember Dad telling me that her favourite Bible story was The Parable of the Talents. As far as she was concerned, it was all about using the gifts God has given you as much as you possibly can. I asked him once if Gran had minded him becoming a hairdresser. I mean, even today people are forever making jokes about it.

'No, she was very enlightened,' he'd said. 'And she could see I'd got a talent for it. I cut *her* hair from being about twelve. By the time I was fourteen, I was even cutting some of her friends' hair. As far as my mother was concerned, if that was what I was good at, then that was what I should do.'

I thought about my talents. They aren't so obvious as Dad's; in fact, they're not obvious at all. Ben would probably say that all I'm good at is talking! Gran packed so much into her life; it was a real inspiration. I went home that night determined to work harder at my GCSEs and to make the most of my life. After all, you never know how long you've got!

There was one thing bugging me, however. Mrs Charming Peterson was at the funeral but neither Mr Peterson nor Chas was. It was during school-time, of course, but I was still surprised. We've spent lots of Sunday afternoons with them so they all know Gran very well.

Mrs C came fussing up to apologize.

'I'm so sorry that my husband and Charles aren't here,' she said. (She must have been feeling tense; nowadays, she rarely calls Chas Charles.) 'It's a busy time on the estate and I gave Charles the choice – I didn't want to force him to come.'

'That's quite all right,' said Mum. 'We totally understand.'

Well, she might but I don't. I think it was downright rude of Mr Peterson – I'm sure he could have got away for the service, even if he didn't stay for the tea. Maybe he and Mrs C are getting on so badly that he couldn't even face sitting next to her in church! Come to think of it, she did look very tired and peaky. Black doesn't suit her. She should have stuck to her usual navy. As for Chas, it's all part of his new image, I suppose. Cool and hard and wanting nothing to do with church or me. I'm furious with him though; he should have come, just out of respect for Gran.

You may be thinking that things have improved with Belladonna. She has, after all, showed glimmers of kindness in the past couple of weeks, mostly to Ben, of course. After that crazy trip that Dad made to pick her up from her party, he and Mum made it very clear that such a thing must never happen again. And it hasn't. She moans, of course, every time she has to make transport arrangements, but she always finds some sad loser who's prepared to give her a lift. She's also much better with the babies. She pulls dreadful faces when she's changing nappies but at least she can do it properly now. And she's got some idea how to keep them happy too.

Mostly it involves food but that's better than nothing. Tonight, however, proved what a low-down skunk she can be.

During the funeral, she was stationed in the church crèche. Mum and Dad wanted the babies with them during the service but needed back-up if they started to be difficult. As it happened, they weren't. Comet went to sleep and Hayley, who is a very sociable baby, bounced on Dad's knee and beamed at anyone who would smile back. She cheered up the proceedings no end. So all Belladonna had to do was read her magazines and put her feet up. She didn't even offer to help the ladies from the Mothers' Union clear up, although she had no trouble eating a very substantial tea. Ben and I washed up, of course. Belladonna spent the time flirting with the young secretary of the CND group. No one wanted to cook later that evening and we sent out for pizzas once the babies were asleep – so apart from a bit of baby-minding in the morning, Belladonna had a very laid-back day.

It was a shock then, when she announced that she intended to take a few days off.

'I am sure you understand,' she said. 'I have worked very hard for the last few days and I am exhausted.'

My eyes were on stalks; I simply couldn't believe she had the cheek or the insensitivity. *She* was exhausted? How did she think Mum and Dad felt? And now she was proposing to leave them in the lurch when they still needed her desperately! I was tired and emotional too. That's my excuse.

'You've got be joking,' I blurted out. 'You've hardly done a thing compared with the rest of us. Every evening you've been slobbing in front of the TV or going out with your friends! You've done a bit extra in the daytime but Dad said he'd pay you for that – so what's your problem? Exhausted? Maybe you should try going to bed earlier!'

'I was not talking to you, Kate,' snapped Belladonna. 'I was talking to Jo and Phil.'

'Yes, Kate,' said Dad. 'That was quite uncalled for. However, Belle, although I appreciate that you have worked a little harder than usual over the last few days, this really isn't a very good time for you to have a break. I'm going to have to work late in the evenings to keep my regular clients happy and you know that there's a backlog of washing and ironing because we've all been so busy with the funeral.'

'Nevertheless,' said Belle, looking rather proud of the word, 'I need a break.'

Dad looked at Mum. She sighed. 'I suppose I can manage,' she said. 'We'll catch up with all the housework eventually and Ben and Kate can help out in the evenings with the babies.'

I couldn't believe it! Mum just isn't herself these days. Why didn't she just tell Belle where she got off? I was about to open my big mouth but I caught Dad's eye and thought better of it.

'Only for a few days though, Belle,' Mum continued. 'Have you arranged with a friend to go and stay somewhere?'

Belle looked blank.

'Oh no,' she said. 'I am going to stay here.'

'Here?' I exploded. I simply couldn't stay quiet any longer. 'Here? You mean you thought you'd just swan around here in your bathrobe like it was a health club or something? Were you expecting your meals brought up to you, by any chance?'

'Kate, that's enough,' said Dad. If he hadn't been so worn out, he'd have sent me to my room, I'm sure. Unfortunately, realizing just how exhausted he and Mum were made me even more infuriated with Belladonna.

Belladonna looked puzzled. 'No, Kate. I would have my meals with you as normal. I would just like to rest for a few days, that is all.'

'I see, so Mum cooks your meals while you do nothing, is that it? Not even Ben or I get away with that! We all have chores to do!'

To my surprise, Ben backed me up. I thought he was too besotted with Belle to care what she did. 'Yeah,' he said. 'That wouldn't be fair. We never get a few days' rest. Even in the holidays we have to do chores.'

'Oh Ben,' said Mum. 'Don't you start as well. Look, why don't you two go somewhere else for a few minutes while your dad and I sort this out?'

Ben stood up. 'I'm off to bed anyway,' he said. 'I'm shattered.'

'I'm going nowhere,' I said. 'I can't believe you two are going to let her get away with this.'

'Kate, please,' said Mum. 'You're overwrought. It really isn't such a big deal. We've all had a tiring few days and you're not helping. Please go to bed. *We're* employing Belle and *we* can sort it out.'

'If you let her have a few days off, then don't expect me to help you,' I snarled. 'She's done far less than me and I'm the one whose gran has died. I'm exhausted too; if she has a break, then I should have one too. For goodness' sake, she gets paid, doesn't she?'

'Only pocket money,' Belladonna butted in.

'It's better than nothing!'

'Kate, go to bed,' said Dad, his voice dangerously quiet. He'd drawn some reserves of energy from somewhere and I could see that he was seriously angry. 'Don't argue,' he said. 'Just go.'

'I like that,' I said, ignoring his last remark. 'She's the one behaving like a selfish brat and you're getting angry with me! You are *so* unfair!'

Dad rose from his chair. He's never hit me but for one awful moment, I thought he might do then. I shot out of the kitchen and slammed the door. From upstairs, I heard a baby whimper. Good, I thought viciously. And I'm not going to do anything about it. I'm not doing anything to help until that useless bimbo has finished her break.

'You've always said you try to be fair,' I yelled at the door. 'Well, you're useless – the worst parents ever! You care more about your stupid au pair than you do about me! "Do not exasperate your children", it says in the Bible. Or didn't you notice that bit?'

Then I ran up the stairs and flung myself on my bed, where I burst into a storm of sobs. It took me a long time to calm down, longer even than Comet whom I'd thoroughly woken up.

Now I feel horrible. My eyes are sore, my head is

throbbing, my mouth's all furry, my stomach's churning and writing about it isn't making me feel any better.

GO HOME, BELLADONNA. GO HOME. I HATE YOU, I HATE YOU, I HATE YOU.

Still no better. Am no longer Kate Lofthouse. Am totally and utterly Wednesday Addams.

Nobody came to talk to me about my horrible behaviour. Usually, when I've opened my big mouth and said far more than is really helpful, Mum or Dad comes and talks to me about it. Well, this time they didn't. Which, in my opinion, just goes to prove what pathetic, useless parents they've turned into.

Vicky didn't agree.

'They were probably just too exhausted to bother,' she said. 'They'd just buried your gran, for goodness' sake. They must have been feeling dreadful – yes, I know you were too. Of course Belladonna is selfish – but that doesn't mean you have to be as well.'

I glowered at her. 'Whose side are you on?' I demanded.

'Yours, of course,' she said. 'I just don't want you getting into some horrible row with your parents when there's no need.'

'You sound like a teacher,' I growled. 'You'll be telling me to grow up or something next.'

'Sorry, I'm sure,' said Vicky. 'I'm only trying to help.'

Ben was equally unsympathetic.

'You're being pathetic!' he shouted when I refused to take

Rover for his evening walk and stomped off towards my room.

'Oh, leave her,' I heard Mum sigh. 'I really can't be bothered with these teenage huffs. Let's just hope she grows out of them soon.'

I put my head back round the door.

'This is not a teenage huff,' I snarled. 'This is a civilized protest about unfair treatment.'

'It's a huff,' said Ben.

'No, it isn't,' I insisted.

'Yes, it is,' said Ben. 'You don't really care about what's fair, you're just jealous of Belle.'

'No, I'm not,' I retorted.

'Yes, you are. It's not fair to Mum to be a pain when Dad's having to work late and Belle's having a break – and we're all feeling lousy about Gran – but you don't care, do you?'

'Oh stop it, you two,' said Mum, her voice quivering. 'I really can't cope with arguing on top of everything else. I'm sure Rover can manage without an evening walk for once.'

That made me feel really bad, of course. I can't bear it when Mum cries; she hardly ever does but she's been doing it a lot lately. And Rover didn't help by sitting with his nose pressed against the back door, thumping his tail.

'*I'll* take Rover out,' said Ben. 'I'll ring Suzie and see if she wants to come.'

Just at that moment, Belladonna came clattering down the stairs.

'I am sorry,' she said. 'Is there a problem with taking Rover out for his walk?'

'Well... sort of,' said Ben. I just glared at her, mulishly.

'I would be very happy to take him for once,' said Belladonna. 'It is a lovely evening and some air would be very refreshing.'

Mum relaxed visibly. 'Belle, that would be so kind,' she said. 'I would be very grateful indeed.'

'No problem,' said Belladonna, beaming round at us with a swish of her long dark hair. 'Come on, Rover!'

'I doubt if he'll want to go with you,' I muttered but even Rover let me down. That dog has no taste. He bounded out after her as if she was the nicest person he'd ever met. She must have been listening to our every word and calculated her entry for maximum effect. It doesn't matter how horrible she is, she always manages to come up smelling of roses.

What my family doesn't seem to understand is that protesting about unfairness is no soft option. I mean, I haven't exactly spent the evening lolling about enjoying myself instead of taking Rover for a walk and helping with the babies. No mango-scented baths for me! First of all, I was so angry with Ben and Belladonna that I spent ages hammering the whole story into this computer. Then I started on my homework. Part of it was answering some questions on a poem called 'When you are old' by W.B. Yeats. It reminded me of Gran and that made me cry. I wanted to go and find Mum or Dad for a cuddle but Dad was still at work and I could hardly bother Mum. Then I felt angry and bad all over again; I mean, if they were more reasonable, I wouldn't have to be stuck in my room feeling like a social leper, just because I have principles. I felt far too irritated to get on with my work so I decided to go downstairs to make a cup of tea. I wish I hadn't bothered – because now I'm even more infuriated and it'll be a miracle if I get my head together to finish my English homework, let alone my Maths.

When I stomped downstairs, Rover wasn't in his basket. Odd, I thought. Surely Belladonna couldn't still be out with him? Unless, of course, she'd met up with some sad loser who wanted to extend the walk with her. Then I realized there were people talking in the kitchen – Belladonna and...surely it couldn't be... Chas?

OK, OK, I admit it – I was stupid. I didn't think, I didn't pray, I just flung open the door and stalked in.

Two startled faces stared at me. Chas sprang to his feet, almost knocking over the coffee mug which was in front of him. He blushed vividly. 'Kate,' said Belladonna, smoothly. 'I met Chas while I was out with Rover. He was...'

'Skateboarding?' I interrupted. 'Go on – surprise me.' I didn't wait for a reply. Well might Chas blush. Skipping Gran's funeral and then having the cheek to come and chat up our au pair while everyone was busy.

'Kate, are you all right?' asked Belladonna. 'You look as if you've been crying.'

Her voice was kind but she just made me angry. I didn't want to know that I was looking red-eyed and blotchy when she was sitting there looking as if she'd just stepped out of a fashion photo.

'Of course I've been crying,' I snapped. 'That's pretty normal, isn't it? My gran's just died.'

'Kate, I'm…' Chas started but I didn't give him chance to continue. I didn't want to hear his pathetic excuses or his feeble pretence that he wasn't there to eye up Beautiful Belladonna and her bellissimo boobs.

'Why didn't you come to Gran's funeral?' I demanded.

'I…' started Chas.

'Oh, don't bother,' I cut in. 'I know we don't matter any more. We were useful once but you've got new friends now. Something more interesting to do.'

Chas's face flushed even darker. I could see that he was angry now.

'Well, if you don't want to listen…' he said.

'No, I don't think I do,' I replied. 'I think I'd rather you just stuck with your new friends and kept out of my sight.'

'Right,' said Chas. 'I get the message. I know where I'm not wanted. Thank you for the coffee, Belle. It was nice to have a chat. Tell Ben I'll see him around. Maybe he'd like to come up to my place sometime as I'm not wanted here.'

'Of course,' said Belladonna, with a look of such doe-eyed sympathy that I wanted to puke. 'I'm sorry about…'

'Oh, it doesn't matter,' said Chas, with a shrug.

'Call me sometime?' Belladonna swept him a sideways glance under her fluttering lashes.

'Er… 'course,' stammered Chas, suddenly losing his cool. 'Yeah, right.'

Then he turned and walked out, without even saying goodbye to me.

Belladonna clapped her hands slowly.

'Well done, Kate,' she said, 'if that is what you wanted.'

'Oh shut up!' I said. 'And what are you sorry about, anyway?'

'It is too late now,' said Belladonna. 'You did not want to listen.'

Aagh! I am so, so full of vitriol, I'm surprised these keys aren't dissolving beneath my fingers. I found out another meaning for it in Science. Vitriol is some sort of acid. And that's now I feel right now. Like I'm so full of acid that it's literally pouring out of me. If I burn a hole in my bed while I'm asleep, I won't be surprised – that's if I actually manage to sleep, of course.

7

My Mum and the Party

I've given up on my protest. One evening of trying to make my point was enough. With Mum insistent that I was in a teenage huff, Dad not even there to notice and Ben slagging me off, there didn't seem much point. And I don't want to give Belladonna any more opportunities to appear saintly while I look like scum. It feels as if she's won hands down but I'm too fed up to care. In any case, I haven't got the energy to make things difficult; it's easier to just go with the flow.

That might sound really pathetic and wimpish, I admit, but the scene over Gran's flowers seemed to open the floodgates. Most of the time I'm fine but then the slightest little thing – like that poem for homework – sets me off blubbing. And I feel so tired! So, I think, does the rest of the family. We're all wandering round like zombies. Dad's particularly bad. He's caught up with his backlog of clients now but comes in and crashes out in the sitting room the moment he's walked through the door. We keep having to wake him for tea! Mum says he's not sleeping well which is part of the problem and keeps threatening to send him to the doctor for some tablets. What with him moaning at her to go to the doctor for her baby blues and her moaning at him about his sleep problems, they make a really happy pair.

Ben's spending every spare moment at Suzie's. I wish I could escape to Chas's like I used to but that's beginning to feel like it was part of a different life. It's not just Chas who has ceased to exist for me – it's Mrs Charming Peterson too. Things must be really bad. She hasn't even popped round with a cheering casserole or wholesome fruitcake to beef us all up. I'm surprised by how much I miss her – and not just for the fantastic food she makes.

I asked Mum about Mrs Charming today.

'Mum,' I said. 'You remember that day when I burst in and Mrs Peterson was really upset?'

'Yes,' said Mum, warily.

'Well, I just wondered if things were all right again now. Is she a bit happier?'

Mum looked shifty, obviously weighing up what she could tell me.

'It's all right,' I said. 'If it's private, I don't need to know.'

Mum shook her head. 'Things aren't good,' she said. 'But she doesn't want people to find out. The best thing you can do is pray for her, Kate.'

'But pray what?' I said. 'I can't very well pray for her if I don't know what's wrong, can I?'

'Oh, I think you can,' said Mum. 'God knows what the situation is, after all. You can just tell God that you care and ask for his blessing on her.'

'What's the point, if he knows what the problem is anyway?'

'Kate, the cleverest person on earth couldn't really tell you how prayer works or why it's important,' said Mum. 'But I find it useful – it certainly helps *me* deal with problems and I'm often surprised by the impact my prayers have on other people.'

'Even when you don't know what you're praying for?'

'You know how sometimes you pour out your troubles to a friend?'

'Yeah,' I said.

'They don't know what to say and you're not even sure they've really grasped the problem?'

'Mmm,' I said. 'I think I know what you mean.'

'Well, why does that help? Why on earth should it?'

I shrugged. 'It doesn't always.'

'No – but it often does. Something changes.'

'Yeah... OK... sort of.' I still wasn't convinced.

'Oh, I know it's not a brilliant comparison,' said Mum. 'But what I'm trying to say is that you can't expect to understand exactly how prayer changes things or why – you can only observe that it often does. Honestly. Even when you're not sure what to pray for.'

So I keep praying for Mrs Peterson. And Mr Peterson, of course. Whatever it is that's wrong, I'm sure it's affecting him too. I suppose I ought to pray for Chas as well but just thinking about him makes the red mist descend. I've had so much grief about him over the last couple of years – it's been like a rollercoaster – and now I've been well and truly dumped. Well, if he's really decided he's had enough of me, I guess it's better that way. More peaceful, at any rate. But I don't see why I should pray for him – especially when he seems to be giving up on church. You can't expect God to do much for you if you're not doing anything for him, can you? Well, I don't think so anyway. That would be seriously unfair.

Surprise! Greg has invited me to his birthday party! People have been talking about it for ages. His parents run a kennels and dog training centre so it's going to be in the big training barn. The music can be really loud because it's quite isolated and his parents aren't even going to be there. They live in a house close by so someone can get them if there's a problem.

I wasn't sure if I wanted to be invited or not. Greg's one of those people who I can't make up my mind about. Sometimes he seems really kind, like when Gran had just died, and other times – I'm not so sure. I don't tend to like the people he hangs around with either. Most of the other girls wanted to be invited because they fancy Greg. Vicky and I have lived through that phase and come out the other side. I thought it would be nice to be invited – good for my street cred – but I couldn't quite see Mum and Dad agreeing to let me go and I didn't want another argument.

So if Greg hadn't invited me, I could have lived with it. But he did.

'You must come, Kate,' he said. 'It'd cheer you up a bit. You've been fed up ever since your Gran died. I mean, I know that's really hard but life goes on.'

He smiled his devastating smile, the one I think I'm proof against.

'Err…' I mumbled.

'Oh come on, Kate! Don't tell me vicars' kids don't do parties!'

'I'd love to,' I said, weakly. And then, 'Have you invited Vicky too?'

'Oh, bring her along if you want to,' he said casually. 'The more the merrier. Just be there, OK?'

When I reported this conversation to Vicky later, she wasn't impressed.

'You know he's dumped Carly, don't you?' she said.

I did and hadn't been able to prevent myself gloating a bit. Greg had moved in on Cute Carly (sorry, I've always called her that because she's a kind of wannabe Barbie doll) just when I'd thought he was going to move in on me! And Cute Carly had been Chas's only serious girlfriend too. I couldn't quite forgive her for any of that.

'So?' I said. 'What's that got to do with it?'

'Oh wake up and smell the roses, Kate!' said Vicky. 'Why's Greg inviting *you*? Not being rude but you're not one of his gang are you?'

'It's a big party,' I said. 'He's inviting loads of people.'

'He wasn't inviting me until you asked him to. He's always fancied you, Kate. I know he's been going out with Carly and I don't expect you're the only girl who gives him the hots – but I bet anything, that's what this is all about.'

'Don't be silly, Vicky,' I retorted. 'He knows I'm not his type.'

'He probably sees you as a challenge. Or maybe it's some silly dare with one of his mates – I don't know. But I should just be careful, if I were you. Make sure he doesn't spike your drink.'

'Vicky, that's ridiculous,' I protested. 'This is just a party in a barn. We're not going to some seedy night club or anything.'

Vicky raised her eyebrows. 'Kate,' she said. 'Sometimes you are so naive I don't know how you survive.'

She was right of course. I am naive. To my amazement, Mum and Dad agreed to me going to the party. Mum wasn't sure at first.

'I don't know...' she said. 'How can Greg's parents supervise the party if they're in the house and you're all in the barn? It seems a bit risky to me.'

'I think she should go,' said Belle, to my surprise. 'Kate needs something to cheer her up; she is still very sad.'

'I'll ask your dad,' said Mum. 'Let's see what he thinks.'

Dad agreed with Belle.

'Belle's right,' he said. 'It would do Kate good. Something different to think about.'

'But…' I said, 'I'm not even sure I want to go.'

'That's exactly why I think you *should* go,' said Dad. 'A couple of months ago, you wouldn't have dreamed of refusing. I know you're still grieving for your gran – we all are – but life goes on. Go to this party. Enjoy yourself. Live a little. There's no harm in that.'

No harm in that. Maybe Dad's a bit naive too.

The party got off to a good start. Dad had done wonders with my hair and Vicky's. We looked as good as we were ever going to. The barn looked great too. Greg and his parents must have worked hard decorating it. I remembered the last time I had been there – for puppy training with Rover. Even now, months later, I felt myself blushing as I remembered the large puddle he had made on the floor and the greed with which he had scoffed all the dog treats. There wasn't a dog in sight tonight of course. The barn was filled with flashing lights and music. Balloons and streamers decked the walls and large tables ran the length of one side, piled with plates of nibbles, bottles of drink and glasses.

'Remember what I said,' said Vicky. 'It's pretty dark in here. Just watch your drink, OK?'

'I'm sure I'll be fine, Vicky,' I said. 'I'm a big girl now.'

'Mmm…' said Vicky. 'And Greg's a big boy too. And you know what *they're* like.'

'Oh stop fussing, Vicky,' I said. 'Come on – let's dance.'

Very few people were already dancing but I didn't care and Vicky let me drag her after me. I hate parties where you stand

97

around and chat, struggling to make yourself heard and getting a sore throat. If there's music, why not dance? Last time I was at a disco, Chas got in a stress with me because I didn't dance with him; at least I didn't have him to worry about this time. I didn't even know if he'd been invited and I was quite relieved that I couldn't see him anywhere. My worries about coming had melted away. Belle was right, though it was an effort to admit it; I needed to get out more. I'd been wallowing far too long. The music was already beginning to make me feel better.

It's a funny thing but once you get a few people having a good time on a dance floor, even if it's one stained with dog pee, it doesn't take long before a lot more join them. There was soon a big gang of us out there, mostly girls of course. Then Chris, a nice enough bloke from my Maths set, came sidling over and asked if he could join me so I made a space. I remembered being a bit snappy with him at the school disco, so I smiled my 'lovely-of-you-to-ask-me-but-don't-get-any-funny-ideas' smile. Right then, I wanted a good night out, not some boy I hardly knew trying to persuade me into a corner. The smile was getting a bit stiff after a couple of tracks so I excused myself and went to find a drink.

Mindful of what Vicky had said, I searched for an unopened bottle. I was struggling with the cap when Greg came strolling over to me, an open can in his hand.

'Lemonade, Kate?' he asked. 'Wouldn't you like something a little stronger?'

'No thanks, I'm fine,' I said and turned to walk away.

Greg laid his hand on my arm.

'Wait, Kate!' he said. 'Will you dance with me?'

He was very close and I could still feel the imprint of his fingers on my arm. Suddenly, my heart was racing. Even though Vicky and I had decided last term that he was the sort of boy who collects girls like scalps, I couldn't help feeling slightly dizzy and weak at the knees. He was still one of the most attractive boys in our year.

'I want to finish my drink,' I said.

'That's OK,' said Greg. 'I need to finish mine too.'

Rats! I thought. I just didn't need the complication of fending off Greg.

'I'm glad you came,' said Greg. 'I thought you might not.'

'My mum wasn't too keen,' I said, 'but Dad thought I needed to get out – and we have this new au pair, Belle. She said I should come. I don't like her very much but she has been a bit nicer since Gran died.'

'I know her,' said Greg. 'She's friends with some of the lads from the rugby club. She said she might come along later.'

I nearly dropped my drink. The last thing I wanted was Belladonna seeing what I was up to at a party. She'd probably think I was a complete loser unless I was making out with a boy. Well, at least I could be seen dancing with Greg. If she had agreed to come to his party, she must think he was reasonably cool.

I knocked back the rest of my lemonade.

'Come on then,' I said. 'Let's dance!'

I glanced round quickly to check on Vicky. She was dancing

happily with the boy from our Maths set. That was OK then; at the school disco, she'd been so miserable that she'd ended up crying in the playground.

Half an hour later, though, she followed me into the loos.

'What did I tell you?' she said. 'Are you just stringing him along – or what?'

'Belle's coming later,' I explained. 'He told me.'

'So?' said Vicky. 'What's that got to do with it? You don't fancy Greg. It's not fair to lead him on, even if he is a slimeball.'

'You're sounding like my mother,' I said. 'I'm not leading him on – I'm just dancing with him! If he thinks that means I fancy him, then more fool him!'

Vicky shrugged. 'Suit yourself,' she said. 'Just don't say I didn't warn you.'

'Warn me about what?' I demanded, although really I knew very well.

'Oh, use your imagination,' said Vicky and left me still adjusting my mascara.

When I came out of the loos, it was flattering to find Greg waiting for me. He held out a glass.

'Another drink?' he said.

'You must be joking!' I laughed. 'Do you want me to spend all night in the loo?'

'Certainly not,' said Greg. 'I want you to spend it with me, of course.'

With the fingers of one hand, he nudged me gently back to the dance floor. I shivered slightly.

'Cold?' he said, all concern.

I said nothing. You, I thought, are just far too smooth. But I'll put up with you for tonight – just until Belle arrives.

At that moment, there was a commotion at the door. A whole gang of new people had just arrived. I recognized them immediately. Not personally – just the look of them. The black and grey T-shirts. The baseball caps. I wondered if there was a pile of skateboards in a heap outside the door. Unable to help myself, I scoured the crowd for Chas. He was there, all right. And so, directly behind him, were Lisa and her best friend Donna. They were like camp followers. I would have felt sorry for them if they hadn't irritated me so much. I mean, haven't they anything better to do than hang round a bunch of boys while they try to do skateboard tricks? How sad is that?

Greg swore.

'Didn't you invite them?' I said.

'Yes,' said Greg, 'but look at the state of them! They're tanked up already!'

'How can you tell?' I said. 'They're always rowdy.'

'Believe me, Kate. They've had a skinful down at the park already.'

I stared across the barn at Chas. He didn't look much different from usual but it was hard to tell at that distance. He was towards the back of the group, Lisa suspiciously close to his side. He did seem to be nodding and smiling at her more than usual; he tends to be shy and quiet in big groups – did that mean he'd already knocked back a few beers?

As a group, the skaters moved in on the food and drink.

'I wasn't sure whether to invite them,' said Greg. 'But I reckoned they'd probably turn up anyway. Better to have them in a good mood, I thought. I just hope they don't cause any trouble.'

I couldn't imagine Chas causing any trouble – but that was the old Chas, the one who seemed to have disappeared for good. Maybe this stranger would down all the alcohol, go looking for a fight and finish the night out cold.

I didn't want to think about it.

'Come on, Greg,' I said. 'Let's dance.'

By half past ten, I wanted to go home. I couldn't help watching Chas out of the corner of my eye. He wasn't dancing. He seemed to be spending all his time hovering beside the drinks table, with Lisa at his elbow. I wondered if Belle was going to turn up. Dancing with Greg was OK but I didn't want him to get the wrong idea. Suddenly I decided that this was ridiculous. Why was I dancing with a boy I didn't really like just so that our au pair would see me with him? Why did I care? The person I cared about most was at that moment spluttering into his drink, over some stupid remark made by the girl I liked least in the entire world! Why was I letting this happen?

'Excuse me, Greg,' I said. 'There's something I have to do.'

Then I stalked across the room, intent on speaking to Chas. OK, so our last meeting had been a disaster but now was as good a time as any to sort it out. Vicky broke away from the boy she was dancing with to join me.

'Kate, I should leave that bunch alone,' she said. 'They're pretty tight – and you know how unpleasant Lisa can be even on a good day.'

I hesitated. I hadn't really had much contact with the skater bunch since that awful day when Mum had given them a lift home – our paths didn't really cross – but they made me nervous. And Lisa made me very nervous. We had history.

But some crazy instinct made me want to at least make contact with Chas. I would ask him to dance – show him that I'd forgiven and forgotten and was sorry too. 'Don't be afraid of your enemies; always be courageous.' That's what Mum always says – some random bit of the Bible, of course. Then she usually adds, 'Imagine them in their underwear – it works for me.'

I was just deciding I really didn't want to imagine the skater crew in their boxers when two weird things happened.

Lisa was laughing up into Chas's face. To my astonishment, in one movement, he put his can on the table and pulled Lisa towards him. Then he kissed her – and not just a peck on the cheek either.

I stood transfixed, clonked and jostled by the other dancers, as conspicuous as a lighthouse in a heaving sea. I thought I might throw up. How could he? How could Chas, who knew only too well how foul Lisa could be – only a few months ago, she had written him a letter, trying to blacken my name – be snogging her before my very eyes?

It was a good job Vicky was on the case. I felt her hand on my arm.

'Don't even think about it!' she hissed. 'You do not want to make a scene.'

Right then, that's exactly what I did want to do. I wanted to march right over there, claw Lisa out of Chas's arms and scratch her eyes out. Cat fight? Yeah, you bet! Fortunately, Vicky wouldn't let me.

'Just leave it, Kate!' she hissed. 'People are beginning to notice.'

I was saved by the second weird thing. Donna, Lisa's best friend, had been leaning against the table. At that moment, her knees buckled and she collapsed onto the floor.

No one in her group seemed to notice. Maybe they were all almost as drunk as she was. I did the first thing to enter my head.

'Chas!' I shouted. 'Look! Donna's fainted!'

'Fainted?' said Vicky. 'You must be joking! Honestly, Kate – what *are* you like?'

Vicky pushed ahead of me and crouched down beside Donna. I couldn't hear her above the music but she seemed to be talking into Donna's face. Then she slapped her cheeks and put her ear to her mouth.

'What's wrong with her?' I demanded. A small shocked group had gathered round by now.

Vicky shrugged. 'What do you expect?' she said. She turned to Chas and Lisa who had, to my relief, disentangled themselves. 'How much has she had to drink?'

Lisa looked embarrassed. 'Not an awful lot,' she said. 'Well, I don't think so anyway.'

Vicky was brisk and business-like. 'Help me turn her on her side,' she said. 'I have to put her in the recovery position. Someone call an ambulance.'

'An ambulance?' said Greg. 'I was going to call my mum!'

'Just get an ambulance!' insisted Vicky. 'She's out cold. Call your mum as well if you like. And get them to turn the music down a bit – then I wouldn't have to keep shouting.'

'Does she really need an ambulance?' queried Greg.

'Yes!' snapped Vicky. 'We don't know what she's drunk or how much!'

'Her uncle's a paramedic,' I said. 'Just do what she says.'

At that very moment, I heard a voice I recognized only too well.

'What's going on here?' said BGM. 'Let me through, please.'

I couldn't believe it. 'What on earth are *you* doing here?' I demanded.

'Picking you up, of course!' said Mum. 'It's eleven o'clock.'

'The party finishes at *twelve!* ' I hissed. 'I *told* you!'

BGM shook her head. 'Rubbish, Kate!' she said. 'I would never have agreed to twelve. But never mind that now – what's wrong with this girl?'

Vicky leaped to her feet. 'Has anyone called an ambulance yet?' she demanded.

There was a worried muttering from the crowd. Now almost everyone in the barn seemed to be gathered round Donna who was still unconscious.

'Greg's gone for his mum,' someone said. 'Maybe he phoned first.'

'It's OK,' said Chas, from somewhere behind me. 'I've phoned.'

'So what's wrong with her?' Mum asked, urgently. 'Is she epileptic or something?'

'I think it's just too much to drink – or mixed drinks or something,' said Vicky, 'but I don't know. She's breathing all right but she's not coming round.'

'No broken bones or anything then?' said Mum. 'I could whip her straight down to hospital in my car.'

We were all hesitating, wondering what was the best thing to do when a boy came bursting in through the door of the barn.

'Somebody come and help!' he yelled. 'There's a gang of yobs outside and they're beating up Greg!'

8

My Mum
Rescues Greg

For a moment, we all stood stock still as if paralysed. Then Mum got to her feet, squared her shoulders and said, 'We'll soon see about that!' And she marched out of the barn.

There was another pause while we all looked at each other, stunned. Then my brain clicked into gear. Vicky would stay with Donna, I knew, and there was an ambulance on its way.

'Chas, ring the police,' I said. 'I'm going to get Greg's parents.'

That was what I intended anyway. When I shot out of the barn door, I was brought up short by the sight that met my eyes, starkly lit by the barn's security lighting. Struggling to his feet, blood streaming from his nose, was Greg. A short distance away, a bigger boy lay in the gravel, curled up like a baby and whimpering. Mum meanwhile was holding a smaller lad at arm's length, one hand at his throat, the other raised as if she was about to punch him. Huddled together, a few metres away, was a small group of young people. Belle, her face white and horrified, was among them.

'Well?' Mum challenged the boy who was struggling to lash out at her. 'Are you going to calm down now?'

The boy still flailed in Mum's grasp. The occasional swear word burst out of him but he obviously didn't have much breath left to speak. With what must have been a terrific effort, he spat at Mum.

At that, one of the boys with Belle sprang forward.

'Stop it, Lee, you idiot!' he said. 'Don't you know who she is? She's a vicar!'

The boy called Lee seemed to go loose in Mum's grasp. For a moment I thought she had strangled him. Maybe she thought so too. Maybe she thought his friend's words would have an impact. Or maybe she was just tiring. Whatever. She must have slackened her grip. The boy tore at her hands and was free. The next moment, he had leaped at her, she lost her footing and they were both wrestling in the gravel.

It was as if a switch had been flicked. Everyone closed in, all trying to haul Lee off BGM – everyone except me, that is. I was too stunned. In the distance, I could hear a siren, whether ambulance or police I didn't know. Help was on its way but I didn't know how long it would be. I ran to get Greg's parents.

I met them as they were hurrying through their garden gate, two of their huge Newfoundland dogs loose at their sides.

The sound of sirens was loud and clear now.

'What's wrong?' demanded Greg's dad. 'I just rang Greg on his mobile and he didn't answer. And what's all that noise?'

It would take too long to explain.

'Just come quickly,' I gasped and turned to run back.

Greg's parents didn't argue but his mum spoke to the dogs and the next moment they were off, barging past me and racing down the path to the barn.

When we arrived, hard on the heels of the dogs, the yard in front of the barn looked like the set for a kids' action movie. Centre stage, cowering on the ground, straddled by a huge, growling dog, was Lee. Not far away, his friend had struggled to sit up but otherwise hadn't moved. A paramedic crouched beside him. Greg was sitting stage left, staunching his nose with tissues and surrounded by cooing girls and the other dog which was enthusiastically licking his face. In the background, Donna was being stretchered into an ambulance while Mum was leaning on a concerned looking Chas and holding something to her lip. There was no sign of Lisa – trust her to disappear as soon as things started to look nasty – but Belle was sobbing her heart out stage right. The rowdies she had brought with her suddenly seemed remarkably subdued and sober.

'Good grief,' gasped Greg's dad. 'What on earth has been going on?'

At that moment, a police car drew up at the yard gates and two officers stepped out.

'Oh no,' said Greg's mum, faintly. She pushed past me. 'Where's Greg?' she said. 'Is he all right?'

'He'll be fine,' I said. Right then, I was more concerned about Mum. It wasn't so very long ago that she'd fractured her skull. I didn't think that wrestling with a yobbo would do her any favours, even if he was smaller than her. I started to cross the yard.

Chas came to meet me. I noted the plastic cup of ice in his hand. 'She's all right...' he started but I walked straight past him as if he was invisible. My contrite mood had vanished. If he thought he could make everything all right between us just by dabbing some ice on BGM's bruises, he could think again. How could he? How could he? Despite the startling events of the last fifteen minutes, the image of him snogging that loathsome snake-in-the-grass Lisa was still burnt into the forefront of my mind.

'Mum,' I gasped. 'What on earth did you think you were doing?'

Mum's eyes smiled at me. Her lip, I could see, was too swollen and split to respond. 'Self-defence. Went on a course once,' she managed to say.

'But that wasn't self-defence,' I spluttered. 'That was attacking two yobs!'

'Greg defence then,' she said. 'Same sort of thing. Quick kick where it hurts. Worked a treat on him.' She nodded at Lee's friend who, at the sight of the police car, had finally got to his feet. Maybe he was trying to look innocent. Fat chance of that.

Between them, the paramedics and the police sorted everyone out. Greg was put in the ambulance with Donna; I heard later that there was some concern that he might be

110

concussed. Lee and his friend were led to the police car. All around me, kids were on their mobiles, obviously ringing for their parents to collect them early. A police officer approached Mum.

'Madam, we need you to come down to the station to make a statement,' he said. 'If you're all right. Unless there's somewhere up here we can use?'

'My house,' said Greg's dad, springing forward. Greg's mum had gone in the ambulance with Greg. 'That would be more comfortable. And I'm sure Reverend Lofthouse would like a cup of tea.'

The police officer's eyebrows shot up. 'Reverend, is it?' he said. 'Not often you get lady vicars breaking up fights.'

'You'd be surprised what lady vicars do,' mumbled Mum. 'Lead me to the tea.'

I started to follow the adults but Mum stopped me.

'No need for you to come, Kate,' she said. 'This could take some time.' She turned to the others. 'Just a minute... I need to phone someone.'

I thought she was ringing for Dad. Ben isn't really old enough to baby-sit but he could hold the fort for twenty minutes or so while Dad whizzed out to pick me up – that's what I imagined anyway.

Instead BGM phoned Mrs Charming Peterson!

'Mum, I...'

'Ssh! Don't interrupt, Kate. Yes, it's broken up early, I'm afraid. Yes, a bit of trouble. No, I'm fine – just talking to the police. No, nothing too serious, don't worry – but if someone could drop Kate and Belle off that'd be great. I'm so sorry to trouble you but I thought you'd be picking up Chas anyway.'

Great for her, no doubt. I couldn't imagine anything more hellish for me. Should I sit in the front and try hard not to listen while Chas and Belle got close in the back? Or should we drive home in stony silence because I'd chosen the back and no one wanted to speak to me? I couldn't even rely on jolly old Mrs Charming to keep the conversation going, seeing as jolly is a word she seems to have forgotten exists and Mr Peterson is usually as silent as the grave.

I tried again. 'Mum, I really don't mind waiting for you...' I began but Mum cut me short.

'Don't be silly, Kate,' she said. 'You need to get home as soon as possible. Stop making a silly fuss, please. Look, all this talking has started the bleeding again!'

Chas offered his cup of melting ice and Mum grabbed some gratefully, wrapped it in her wad of tissues and pressed it against her lip.

'Come on,' said Greg's dad. 'Let's get on with this. Then I'll give you a lift home – you don't look in any fit state to drive, Reverend Lofthouse.'

With that, Greg's dad, the policeman and Mum started up the path back to the house and I was left in the yard with Chas. Other cars had been arriving and about half the kids had already gone. I looked round for Vicky hopefully and to my relief she came running over.

'Sorry, Kate,' she said. 'I thought I'd better stay with Donna till the ambulance arrived. Is it true what they're saying about your mum?'

'Probably,' I said, managing a rueful smile. 'She did kick one lad rather hard and nearly throttle the other.'

'And then try to punch his lights out on the floor?'

I shrugged. 'Dunno,' I said. 'I went to get Greg's parents. What I want to know is, how did it start?'

'Oh, that's easy,' said Vicky. 'Someone just told me. Belle and her mates turned up just as Greg was running off to get his mum and dad. He told them they couldn't come in because he could see that some of them were really drunk. So two of them got all mouthy and then just launched into him.'

'And the others just stood and watched? Including Belladonna? Typical!'

'No, I did not just stand and watch.' It was Belle, her voice indignant although still snuffly with tears. 'I was shouting and shouting at them to stop – but the others were laughing! Then your mother came out.'

'Good job she did,' I growled. 'Were you just going to stand there and let them kill him – or what?'

'The other boy ran for help. What could I do?'

'You should never have brought them here in the first place,' I said. 'You must have known they were drunk.'

Belle's lips curled contemptuously. 'French boys do not get drunk like you English do,' she said. 'We learn young how to treat alcohol. What do you call your football hooligans? Lager louts?'

'That's got nothing to do with it,' I said, my voice rising

angrily. 'They were drunk, you knew they were drunk and you still brought them to Greg's party.'

'I did not know you cared so much about Greg,' said Belladonna, raising an eyebrow maliciously.

'Oh stop it, you two,' Vicky interrupted. 'The last thing we need is a cat fight. How are you going to get home? Do you need a lift?'

'Mum's arranged a lift with the Petersons,' I mumbled, 'but…'

'You can come with me, Kate,' Vicky said, reading my mind, 'but I'm afraid we haven't got room for you, Belle. We've got to take someone else too.'

I didn't stop to ask who; I just breathed a huge sigh of relief and hurried after Vicky. Her mum's car was waiting close to the gate. There was already someone sitting in the back and Vicky quickly snuggled in next to him. It was Chris, the nice boy from our Maths set. I opened the passenger door and flopped into the seat. This evening had been going on far too long and was far too full of surprises.

'It's all right if we take Kate too, isn't it, Mum?' said Vicky. 'Her mum's having to talk to the police.'

'Of course,' smiled Vicky's mum. 'You all right, Kate?'

I nodded but the kindness in her voice was too much for me. Silent tears started to seep down my face. Vicky's mum said nothing but handed me a tissue. In the back, Vicky and Chris were silent too; I stole a glance over my shoulder and quickly looked away. Chris had his arm round Vicky and her head was resting on his shoulder. I wondered if Belle was crying on Chas's shoulder right now or whether Lisa would be filling my seat in the Petersons' car. Before long, my tissue was nothing but a sodden little ball, hard and lumpy like the sadness and jealousy that was knotting my throat.

When I crawled into bed, I intended to sleep deep into the next morning. It was Saturday so there was no school and no church. Nothing for which I had to get up and look civilized. If my eyes were swollen, my face blotchy and my temper foul, it wouldn't matter; I would stay in my room.

Fat chance. The phone rang at nine o'clock and again at nine fifteen. Then it rang again at nine forty.

I burst out onto the landing.

'What's going on?' I yelled down the stairs. 'Who keeps phoning?'

Ben was coming upstairs.

'Mum!' he shouted. 'It's for you again.'

I heard Mum muttering crossly from her room and then she hurtled out onto the landing, tying her dressing gown belt.

'This is ridiculous,' she huffed. 'Who is it this time?'

'You've gone national,' said Ben, with a grin. 'It's the *Daily Mail*.'

'You're winding me up,' said Mum, her face going ashen.

'No, I'm not,' said Ben. 'They want to speak to the Vigilante Vicar.'

'No... they didn't say that!' Mum was clutching the stair rail now and looked ready to faint.

115

'Oh yes, 'fraid so,' said Ben. 'That's what the reporter called you.'

Mum sat down heavily on the stairs. 'I need some advice,' she said. 'I'd better get in touch with the diocesan press officer. Tell the dratted person they'll have to ring back later. And wake up Belle up. Her holiday will have to end pronto. Phil's at the salon and this is going to be bedlam.'

I winked at Ben. Right then I didn't care if Mum's picture was going to be splashed all over the tabloids under the headline Vigilante Vicar; for the first time in months she had sounded like her old feisty self.

Ben ran back to the phone, I rushed to the bathroom and Mum hurried down to the kitchen where the babies were beginning to cry.

Just then, the doorbell rang. I stopped scrubbing my teeth, dumped my toothbrush in the sink and ran for the door, scenes from the movie *Notting Hill* flooding my brain.

'Don't answer it,' I tried to yell downstairs, foam dripping from my mouth. But I was too slow. Mum had already got there, baby on hip, ancient, grubby dressing gown askew.

Flash! Flash! Pop! Flash! The Vigilante Vicar had been caught on camera by the paparazzi.

9

My Mum Gets to Be Famous

Ever tried living with a celebrity? The novelty wears off pretty soon, I can tell you. At first we tried to laugh about it.

'How silly!' said BGM, when she'd just shut the door after her first photo call. 'Who wants to see a picture of me in my dressing gown with a split lip?'

'Give it a couple of days and it'll all die down,' said Dad when he got home later.

But he was wrong. Anyone would think no one had ever muscled in and broken up a fight before. It was Mum being a vicar that did it, of course. She'd created great headlines for the Sunday papers. Along with VIGILANTE VICAR there was MINISTERING PEACE? and BIBLE BASHER. We thought the last one was quite witty but as time wore on, our patience began to evaporate. Mum seemed to be constantly on the phone and then, worse, she got asked to be on breakfast TV!

'This is ridiculous,' Mum complained. 'I only broke up a

fight. Anyone would have done the same.'

'But "anyone" doesn't preach sermons about non-violence and "turning the other cheek",' said Dad. 'No, love, there's no escape. You'd better do it.'

'But what about the babies?' Mum wailed. 'I can't leave them and go running off to London in the small hours – I'm still feeding them!'

'Take them with you,' said Dad. 'Belle can go with you. Just be careful who finds out that you're breastfeeding twins or they'll make headlines out of that too!'

'Is that all right, Belle?' Mum asked. 'It'd be a very long day but we could pay you extra.'

But Belle has been very subdued since Greg's party. Obviously there was nothing much she could do to stop those lads causing trouble but I think she's really embarrassed looking back on it. I mean, however hard she blustered about lager louts, they were still supposed to be her friends, weren't they?

'That is fine, Jo,' she said. 'It will be no trouble. And I would like to visit a TV studio.'

'Good,' said Dad. 'That's sorted then. I'm married to a media star. Bound to be excellent for business. We'd just better make sure you look good on the day, darling!'

Well, it's all right for him – but what about me? All I need is my outrageous mother sounding off in front of everyone I know over their breakfast. Enough to put anyone off their cornflakes! Embarrassing or what? Oh, OK, I know she's done really well – I ought to be proud of her, catching the media's attention like this. I suppose she's quite a hip-looking vicar really – except when she's wearing her baby-puke stained dressing gown, of course. Dad's always doing something different with her hair colour and she has so many piercings in her ears that I've lost count. She has to choose her earrings carefully these days though. One well-aimed grab from a baby and she could have her ear ripped off! Ouch!

Today was the big day. Mum had to be at the studio at six a.m. so Dad was up with her at three doing her hair. I heard them creeping around but decided I wouldn't go and look. If he'd done something really drastic, I wouldn't be able to get back to sleep for worrying about it. When Dad woke Ben and me later, it was to a strangely quiet house. No baby noises – the twins had gone with Mum. It felt really odd.

'Hurry up!' said Dad. 'She should be on sometime between seven and eight.'

'I'm not sure I want to see,' I groaned. 'What did you do to her hair?'

'Wait and see. You'll like it,' he said.

We don't have a TV in the kitchen – yes, OK, we're weird but what's new? – so for once, we were allowed to take our breakfast into the sitting room. Rover thought that was very exciting – he always has an eye for a potential food accident. I, on the other hand, suddenly had no appetite at all.

Just wondering what sort of an idiot BGM would make of herself had turned my stomach.

The clock hand crept closer and closer to eight.

'They'd better hurry up,' said Ben,' or we're going to be late.'

'So am I,' said Dad,' but people will understand.'

'Oh, for goodness' sake – it's not such a big deal,' I snorted.

'So why can't you eat your breakfast?' snapped Dad.

'Because the thought of what she's going to say makes me feel s...'

'Shut up!' interrupted Ben. 'They said her name!'

Sure enough, suddenly, there she was, on the screen, large as life and twice as technicolour.

'Good grief,' said Dad. 'Look at that make-up!'

'Looks good,' grunted Ben.

'Looks... different,' I managed.

To my absolute astonishment. Mum looked amazing. Dad had given her a very dark burgundy rinse. It was all gloss and spikes.

'At least their hairdressers have left her alone,' he said, approvingly. 'That's *my* handiwork, I'll have you know. My most expensive serum went on that.'

Beneath her spiked hair, the make-up artists had done serious work with eye-liner and mascara.

'She looks like an Ancient Egyptian!' said Ben.

'More Goth, I think,' said Dad.

'No, Bollywood,' I said.

Whatever. She looked stunning. We were all so amazed, we missed the first part of what she was saying completely. When we caught up with her, she was deep in discussion about the problems of practising your faith in today's society. It was all familiar stuff to us; I mean she rants on about it all the time. The presenter, however, seemed fascinated. Dad was nodding approvingly and I was just thinking this wasn't too bad after all when the presenter said:

'Well, Jo, it's been very interesting to have you on the show. Just before we leave, can I ask one last question?'

'Of course,' said BGM.

The presenter leaned forward and gave Mum a gooey smile.

'For all the larger ladies watching, can I ask you how comfortable you feel with having an alternative body shape?'

'What's that mean?' asked Ben.

'What a cheek! Slap her, Jo!' shouted Dad.

I watched Mum's face tighten. Oh no, I thought. Oh no.

Mum smiled sweetly. She too leaned forward.

'Well dear,' she said. 'If by that you mean, do I like having a big bum, no I don't. It's comfortable to sit on, but that's about all. I cope with it, of course – I wouldn't let something as trivial as that screw me up – God made me as I am. But if you think I don't sometimes wish God had made me a size 10 instead, then get real – of course, I do! And I expect you do too, don't you?'

'Brilliant!' gasped Dad. 'But the church press office isn't going to like it.'

'I don't get it,' said Ben.

'I'll explain,' I said. 'Come on, Ben. We'll be late for school.'

Right then, I didn't want to go to school – what on earth would people say? But I didn't want to stay still either. Really, what I wanted to do was run around screaming for a bit.

Getting to school quickly, finding Vicky and bending her ear felt like the only attractive alternative.

Vicky, as ever, was sympathetic and sensible.

'She was brilliant,' she said. 'I don't know why you're embarrassed. I wish I could think that quickly under pressure. Some of these TV presenters need to be told where to get off. And she looked *fantastic!*'

'But what will everyone else think?' I worried. 'You're always on our side anyway. I mean, basically she told that presenter she was overweight – in front of millions of viewers! Won't she get sued or something?'

'Doubt it!' said Vicky 'I mean, she didn't say anything that wasn't true. And that presenter's going to look a bit of a sad loser if she makes a fuss. I mean, what's she going to say? "That nasty vicar implied I wasn't a size 10"?'

'I suppose you might be right,' I said.

'Of course I am,' said Vicky. 'You just wait and see.'

She *was* right, of course. There's something about appearing on TV that's like magic. Suddenly, everyone seemed to think BGM could take on the Vicar of Dibley. People kept coming up to me and saying how great she'd been. Some girls even said they thought her hair was fantastic and they'd definitely be trying out Dad's salon. Kids who'd always sneered at me because every so often Mum comes into school to take assemblies told me they'd always thought she was cool. I began to feel like a celebrity myself. Even better, Vicky pointed out that however unsettling all this was, at least it seemed to have dragged Mum out of her awful lifeless gloomy phase.

'You'll have to stop calling her BGM at this rate,' she said. 'She didn't exactly look glum this morning.'

'Well, she can go back to being Big *Bum* Mum then,' I said, laughing. 'There's certainly no change there!'

And then, at lunchtime, something happened that took my mind completely off Mum and her TV antics. I should have expected it I suppose – but I didn't.

I've barely seen Chas since Greg's party. Maybe if I'd accepted that lift from his mum, I would – who knows? Whatever. He doesn't seem to be going out with Lisa; in fact, she doesn't seem to be hanging around with his crew any more. But until today, I haven't really paid much attention. I've been too distracted. It's been a real rollercoaster – all the excitement with Mum and all the grief about Gran. I haven't even given Greg much thought, despite dancing with him so much. Silly me. I should have done.

He didn't come to school for a few days after the party and when he did, he still looked a mess. He was lucky – his nose hadn't been broken – but he had some grisly bruising across his face and an impressive black eye. He'd written a thank you letter to BGM and his dad had brought it round with some flowers. She thought it was lovely but I thought it was really sickly – typical smooth-boy Greg. A couple of times, he asked me how she liked being a media star – you could see he was really impressed. But at least he wasn't all over me. It had crossed my mind briefly that he might be.

123

Today, all that changed. Maybe he was waiting for his looks to return; maybe he thinks that's really important. He does look almost normal now apart from a bit of bruising under his eyes which I'm sure he knows gives him an interesting romantic look like Frodo in *The Lord of the Rings*. Or maybe it was Mum being on the telly that did it.

I'd gone out onto the school field for a spot of lunchtime sunbathing, to get away from the endless comments about Mum and to give Vicky a bit of time on her own with Chris. She's great about that, of course, being Vicky.

'You don't need to worry that I'm going to ignore you,' she said, the day after the party. 'I'm going to need you when this all falls apart, aren't I?'

'It might *not* fall apart!' I argued.

'Oh yes, like I'm going to marry him, Kate! He's the first person I've ever gone out with! Anyway, I don't want to turn into one of those boyfriend bores. And I like variety. Who wants to spend all their spare time with the same person?'

That's Vicky. Always thoughtful, always practical. And she's right, of course. Even when things were going really well with Chas, I didn't want to spend all day, every day with him.

But I am trying to give Vicky some space and just then, I really did want some peace and quiet.

It didn't last long. I was suddenly aware that the shade had become deeper. I shivered a bit. Typical. You can never rely on British sunshine for more than twenty minutes. But it wasn't the sun that had gone in; it was Greg who had come out onto the field to find me.

'Hi,' he said when I opened my eyes and peered up at him. 'Mind if I join you?'

(Question: why do people ask stupid questions like that? I mean, what can you say? Yes, I mind deeply. Now please go away?)

I shrugged but stayed lying down. I wasn't going to move.

He sat down beside me. I had my arms folded underneath my head and, to my astonishment, he ran a finger along one of them. That made me sit up, I can tell you!

'Well?' I said. 'What do you want?' No, not exactly welcoming, was it? But he should have kept his hands to himself!

My brusque tone didn't deter him. I don't think anything would deter Greg really; he just thinks he's God's gift to girls.

He sat down close to me – too close.

'Just wondering if you could overlook the fact that I had to be rescued by your amazing celebrity mother the other week – and whether we could continue where we left off that night?'

So – he was embarrassed to have come off the worst in that fight, was he? I mean, how uncool was that? Being saved from a punch-up by the mother of the girl you fancy? Ouch! Well, I'm no stranger to the pain of being embarrassed by BGM. I could afford to be kind – I thought.

'Forget it,' I said. 'It was two against one – you didn't stand a chance. It wasn't your fault.'

He breathed a sigh of relief. 'I don't want to forget the rest though,' he said, his arm stealing behind my back.

'The rest of what?' I said.

'Come on, Kate,' he said, his voice almost a whisper. 'Don't tell me you don't want to go out with me? Not after dancing with me all night?'

I stood up quickly. 'You read too much into things,' I said. 'You're a good dancer – that's the only reason I stuck around you.' I was blushing. It wasn't the complete truth and I suspected he knew that.

'You're winding me up,' he said, jumping to his feet. 'Playing hard to get! Come on, Kate, don't mess me around!'

'I'm not,' I said, backing away. 'You're all right, Greg, but I don't want to go out with you. You're not my type.'

'I don't believe you!' Greg said and, to my astonishment, he made a grab for me, pulling me hard against his chest.

I'm afraid I didn't stop to think – as usual – I just lashed out. Next moment, there was a startling red mark across the side of his face that wasn't bruised. I won't repeat what he said. He staggered back a bit.

'Like mother, like daughter,' he spat. 'Drop dead, Kate, you nasty little…'

'Problem, Kate?'

I whirled round. It was like a scene from an American teen movie. All Chas needed to say was 'This guy bothering you?' and it would have been perfect. I would have giggled if I hadn't felt so awful – awful for hitting Greg and even more awful that Chas had seen me do it.

'Er… no, I'm all right thank you, Chas,' I gasped. 'I… I…' and then I was too embarrassed to stay there any longer. I took to my heels and ran. I didn't stop running until I found Vicky where she was sitting with Chris in the courtyard.

'Vicky,' I panted. 'I've just done the most awful thing. I'm so embarrassed. This time I really am going to die!' And with that, I flung myself at her and burst into tears.

Chris tactfully vanished and Vicky mopped me up and took me to the loos to sort my face out.

'Why did Chas have to be there?' I said, huddled over the sink in anguish. 'Why wasn't he kicking around with his skateboard mates?'

'My fault,' said Vicky.

'Your fault?' I met her eyes in the mirror, astonished.

'He was looking for you. I told him you were on the field.'

'He was *looking* for me?'

'He didn't say why. Just asked me if I knew where you were.'

'But I thought he didn't want to know me any more. I thought...'

'Kate, you don't think, you just react. You know you do.'

Vicky's words hung in the air. She's right, of course. That's always, always, always been my problem. I don't think, I open my big mouth, and... disaster. Mum showed me a bit in the Bible once. It says: 'Just think how large a forest can be set on fire by a tiny flame! And the tongue is like a fire!' Something like that, anyway. It's so right. My tongue is like a blowtorch sometimes! Over the past few weeks, everything I've said to Chas has been the same. Thoughtless. Damaging. Unkind.

I've been burning up our friendship with my very own matches.

'But Chas has been just as bad...' I said. 'He's been nasty too.'

Vicky sighed. 'You said weeks ago that you thought there was something wrong with him – that his mum and dad weren't getting on. Maybe he's got an excuse. Why don't you just *ask* him? Tell him you're really worried. Say you're sorry you've been horrid.'

I nearly went for it. Honestly, I nearly did. I nearly ran off straightaway to find Chas and have it out with him. But then I remembered that scene with him in the den, I remembered him chatting in the kitchen with Belle – it was still all so raw – and I remembered him in that clinch with Lisa.

'No,' I said, grinding my teeth. 'No, Vicky, I can't. I just can't.'

Vicky's shoulders sagged. 'You know what your mum would say, don't you?'

I nodded. I knew only too well what my celebrity mum would say. She even managed to squeeze it onto the telly this morning! *Why don't you just pray about it?* That's her answer to almost everything. And why, oh why, do I virtually never remember until it's too late?

10

My Mum
Sorts Me Out

I thought I could just walk away from hitting Greg. I'd got my message across, hadn't I? As far as I was concerned, that was all there was to it. But Chas wasn't the only witness and Greg, his pride wounded, wasn't the sort to keep quiet and forget about it. People had seen a girl turn him down. People had seen a girl slap him – worse, the girl whose mum had been on the TV that very morning! You didn't do that and get away with it, as I soon found out. There wasn't anything *wrong* with *him*, of course – no girl would *refuse* to go out with him. So there must be something wrong with *me*. The gossip machine got going and by the end of the day, people seemed to have lost interest in my amazing mother and instead were asking me all kinds of personal questions. It was bizarre. When a kid in Year 7 asked me if I'd refused to go out with Greg because really I had no boobs, only padding, I felt like slapping him too!

'Go and wash your mouth out, you rude little boy,' I said and stalked off with my chin (and my boobs) in the air.

It was Lisa (of course) who really managed to dig the knife in. She cornered me in the loos, the scene of a previous showdown between us.

'You haven't stopped lashing out then, Katie?' she said. 'I heard what you did to Greg. Nice – when he's just recovering from nearly breaking his nose. You and your mum – what are you two like? At least she was defending Greg though. Unlike you.'

My mouth opened and shut a few times and I screwed up my fists tight, remembering what Vicky said yesterday and a previous occasion when a tussle with Lisa had put her in the hospital and me in serious trouble. I would not just react, I would not! Dear Lord, I said silently. Please keep me calm. Please help me to say the right thing.

'I'm very proud of my mother,' I said carefully. 'One day I hope to be like her.'

Lisa snorted. 'What, rude and fat, you mean?'

'I meant,' I said carefully, 'I'd like to be kind and brave.'

Lisa's lip curled. 'Way to go, Katie,' she said. 'You'd better keep practising.'

With that, she stalked off and I let my hands unclench. I had dug my nails in so hard that I'd almost broken the skin. My legs were shaking – but at least I hadn't strangled her with her own immaculately straightened hair – which is what she deserved!

When I got home, I was exhausted. I ignored Belle who, as

ever at this time of day, had the babies in their high chairs and was entertaining them with Marmite toast. I slumped down next to Rover in the hall and took his heavy black head in my hands to stroke his lovely, silky ears. He gazed up at me adoringly and licked my face. Why can't boys be as straightforward as dogs? They have all the disadvantages – smelly, messy, always looking for the next snack – and none of the advantages – never take offence, loyal, know their place.

'I don't know, Rover,' I said. 'I can see why people often cry more when their pets die than when their humans do. Loving an animal is so much less complicated.'

Rover thumped his tail and licked me again. I wrapped my arms round him. My head was aching and tears began to trickle down my face and onto Rover's coat. I had been here before, I knew, telling the dog he was easier than people, struggling to understand my feelings. Not six months ago, Mum gave me a tacky little card with some verses from the Bible about love on it. I couldn't remember much now except for one line which had stuck in my head: 'Love always perseveres.' It had helped me at the time. Now, I felt too tired and fed up to be bothered.

What's the use, God? I whispered. Whatever I do, it turns out wrong! And I just don't know what love is. Did I love Gran? She only died a little while ago but I'm getting on with life. OK, so every so often I burst into tears but it's not made a huge amount of difference. Do I love Mum and Dad? Sometimes they annoy me so much I wish they'd drop dead! And what about Chas? He's been so horrible recently and I really despise him for snogging Lisa – but when he saw me hit Greg, I wanted to die.

I hugged Rover harder. 'Oh dear,' I told him. 'I must be a really horrible person. Surely if you really love people you don't spend half your time feeling furious with them?'

Just then, I heard voices in the kitchen. Ben must be home. Before I had chance to move, he'd opened the hall door. He looked down at my tear-stained face and crouched beside me. He patted me awkwardly.

'Greg deserved it,' he said. 'He's a total big-head. Just ignore all the stupid comments. By tomorrow, everyone'll have forgotten – you'll see.'

But that wasn't the point. A huge lump rose in my throat. 'Chas saw…' I blurted. 'Chas saw me… behaving like a *bitch!*'

Ben shook his head. 'Chas saw Greg behaving like a slime-ball. Look, why don't you go and talk to Chas? He hasn't changed really. He's just taken up skateboarding.'

I shook my head. He must have changed. The old Chas would never have snogged someone as nasty as Lisa. 'No,' I said. 'I can't. I just can't.'

Ben shrugged and stood up. 'Pity,' he said and went back into the kitchen.

I felt too drained to move. I lay beside the dog and let him lick my tears away. Sounds gross but I couldn't care less right then.

About five minutes later, the kitchen door opened again.

'Kate, I have brought you some tea.'

It was Belle.

I opened one eye and grunted ungraciously. To my surprise, Belle placed the mug and a plate on the floor beside me and then sat down. The plate held a couple of chocolate biscuits (Ben's idea, probably.)

'Kate, please do not be angry with me for saying this,' Belle started.

My eyes flew open and I stared hard. What on earth was she going to say?

Belle laughed nervously. 'Do you know how scary you can be?' she said. 'You and your mother. You are so alike in some ways.'

I was speechless.

Belle swallowed and carried on. 'I know you do not like me,' she said. 'We got off on the wrong foot – is that what you say?'

I nodded.

'And boys always like me. I cannot help it – so you are jealous too.'

What do you say to that? Her cheek left me breathless!

'But there is something I must say to you. It is important – very important. Will you listen to me, please?'

I pulled myself up to sitting and swigged the tea. 'I'm listening,' I said, glaring at her.

'You are unhappy about Chas,' she said. 'He is very unhappy too. He wants to talk to you but you keep pushing him away.'

'I like that...' I started.

'No, listen, Kate,' said Belle. 'He has talked to me...'

My cheeks started to burn with fury; I couldn't help it. She was right. I couldn't bear the thought of him talking to her –

133

it was worse than him kissing Lisa because, really, I knew that taking Belle into his confidence meant more.

'Kate, you should not be jealous,' Belle continued. 'We can all be friends, if you will let us.'

Oh yeah, like friends nick all your special bath foam and don't replace it, I thought, furiously. Yeah, right.

'But first you should go and talk to him. There is something troubling him.'

'What?' I said. 'If he wants advice over which girl to ask out, I don't want to know. I've been there before and he can forget it.'

'He has not told me what it is,' Belle said. (I breathed a sigh of relief.) 'He only told me that he wanted to talk to you – and that you would not have anything to do with him.'

'So how do you know there's something troubling him, then?'

Belle tossed her beautiful long hair. 'I understand boys,' she said. 'That is all.'

My fingers itched to scratch her eyes out. For cool arrogance, she takes some beating. *Boys like me. I cannot help it. I understand boys. That is all.* Maybe she doesn't understand how that comes across. Maybe it's because she's struggling with the language. I'm attempting to be charitable. Really, I just think she's a big-head.

But she was trying to be kind. Even churned up and infuriated as I was, I could see that.

I took another slurp from my mug. 'I'll think about it, OK?' I said. 'Thank you for telling me – and thank you for the tea and biscuits… Oh!'

'What?' said Belle.

'Look,' I said and pointed to the empty plate.

Rover grinned up at us, a crumby, biscuity grin.

'Bad dog!' said Belle. 'Those biscuits were for Kate!'

But we both laughed and Rover thumped his tail happily. And laughing made me feel a whole lot better.

That night, we all went out for a Chinese meal, even the babies. We know a great baby-friendly restaurant in town and Hayley and Comet are certainly up for chomping through rice and prawn crackers these days. Mum and Dad thought we ought to celebrate. I mean, it isn't everyday you end up on the telly just because you broke up a scrap at a party!

I enjoyed it – sort of. It was great to see Mum in such good form, especially considering she'd been up since three a.m. – her old energy really seems to be coming back. And I always enjoy Chinese food. But at the back of my mind the old problem was niggling away. What was the matter with Chas? What was the matter with Mrs Peterson? What was I going to do about it?

When we got home, it was still quite early but Mum was looking exhausted. The weather was warm and humid which hadn't helped.

'Mum, Ben and I can bath the girls if you want,' I said. 'Then you could go to bed. We can bring them to you when they're ready for their feed.'

Mum's face lit up. 'Would you, Kate? That would be really

kind. I do feel absolutely shattered. Are you sure that's OK with you too, Ben?'

''Course,' said Ben. 'No problem. I was going to ring Suzie but she won't mind if I leave it till later.'

Ben amazes me. How come he manages to make life so straightforward when for me it's like a maze? There he is, only just a teenager, hardly ever gets in a stress, lovely, steady girlfriend and so sensible it's enough to make you puke. Is it just personality or is it that he's actually taken notice of all those words of wisdom we've been drip-fed by Mum and Dad over the years?

Anyway, there's something very uplifting about bathing funny, cuddly babies if you're not too tired and you don't mind getting wet. By the time we'd got them cosily togged up in their sleepsuits, I was feeling relatively relaxed. We took the babies through to Mum and she settled down with them in her bed to feed them.

'Kate, don't go,' said Mum. 'I want to talk to you a minute.'

I was slightly sleepy and unsuspecting. I sat down on the bed next to her and stroked Hayley's warm, slightly damp little head with my finger.

'What is it?' I said.

'I'm worried about you,' she said. 'I haven't been around much the last week or so, I know, but I can see that there's something stressing you out. Want to tell me what it is?'

'I... I... I don't know where to start,' I gasped, completely taken by surprise.

'How about starting with Chas?' said Mum. 'We haven't

been seeing much of him recently.'

She's amazing, isn't she? Drives me round the bend with her words of wisdom, makes a habit of embarrassing me at every possible opportunity, has obviously been feeling rough for several months – and yet still knows exactly what's likely to be on my mind.

'Chas,' I said. 'Oh Mum, I've been so horrible to him – but then he's been horrible to me – and I don't know how to begin to make it better again. Ben and Belle both say I should talk to him – but I can't!'

'Why not?' said Mum.

For the first time, I really openly admitted it. 'I'm jealous,' I said. 'I'm jealous that he's more interested in skateboarding than anything else, I'm jealous that he likes Belle, I'm jealous that he kissed Lisa at Greg's party – I'm so jealous that it really, really hurts. He's *my* friend – he's the first really good friend I ever had. Even when he was going out with Carly he was still *my* friend. When he went to boarding school and we drifted apart that was because of me – it wasn't *him* not being my friend. But now he's got so much else on his mind, there isn't space for me or anything to do with me – he couldn't even be bothered to come to Gran's funeral!'

Mum sighed. 'Where there is jealousy and selfishness, there is also disorder and every kind of evil,' she said.

'Oh please,' I said. 'Don't quote the Bible at me.'

'Sorry,' she said. 'I know it can be irritating. It just seemed so appropriate.'

I groaned. 'Oh go on then. You are the TV vicar, after all.

Say it again.'

'Where there is jealousy and selfishness, there is also disorder and every kind of evil,' she said.

'Selfishness? It isn't selfishness. I'm just jealous,' I said.

'And it isn't selfish to be jealous?' said Mum. 'You want Chas all to yourself. If that isn't selfish, I don't know what is. The green-eyed monster – that's what they call jealousy. Shakespeare, I think – not the Bible for once.'

'But...' I started and then stopped. She was so right. It was obvious when you thought about it.

'Look, Kate, Ben and Belle are right. You need to talk to Chas. He needs you right now; I know he does.'

'It's to do with his mum, right?' A sudden, horrible chill gripped my heart. I've been trying to ignore my suspicions for weeks; I couldn't any longer.

Mum nodded. 'I can't say any more; she made me promise. Look, I'll take you up there tomorrow night if you want.'

I shook my head. 'I'll ring him now,' I said. 'You're right. I'm just being selfish.'

Mum sank back into her pillows, the babies lolling beside her.

'If you're feeling really kind, you could put these two in their cots for me,' she said.

I nodded and scooped up Hayley.

'Guess you don't want any more advice, do you?' said Mum.

'I know what you're going to say,' I sighed. 'You say it all the time. Just pray about it, right?'

Mum smiled. 'Sorry I'm so predictable,' she said.

11

My Mum is Right in the End... as Usual.

I carefully carried Hayley and Comet to their cots and snuggled them in. They look so adorable when they're curled up asleep, it makes you wonder how you can possibly ever be annoyed with them. But one yell too loud when I'm trying to sleep and I could cheerfully throttle them. You see – I'm the same about everyone. I love them, I love them not. Very Wednesday. (Question: do you think the Addams family actually love each other? I mean, Morticia and Gomez smoulder enough to set light to the furniture but is that love?)

Anyway, if I was going to be brave and visit Chas, I decided I'd better get on with it. I hesitated in the hall by the phone. I'd have to ring first; I didn't want to cycle to his house and find he was out skateboarding.

Mrs Charming answered.

'Why, Kate – how lovely to hear your voice! We haven't

seen you for ages. I'm afraid I've been a bit tied up recently, what with one thing and another.'

'I was... er... wondering about dropping by, actually,' I stammered. 'Is... is Chas around?'

'Oh yes, he's here. I'm sure he'd love to see you. Are you coming now?'

'As soon as I can,' I said. 'Thanks. Bye.'

When I put the phone down, my hand was trembling. This was ridiculous. How had it got so difficult just to phone Chas's mum?

I was hauling my bike out of the garage when a voice startled me.

'Hi Kate.'

I spun round.

'Greg!' I said. 'What are *you* doing here?'

He was standing by the gate, two huge dogs sitting obediently at his side.

'I wanted to talk to you,' he said. 'So I thought I'd walk Chloe and Biggles over this way.'

I was flattered of course. But flattered wasn't good enough. Right then, I just wanted to go. I'd told Mrs Charming that I was on my way; having plucked up the courage to speak to Chas, I was desperate to get it over with. And I certainly didn't want to offend him by not turning up. Worse, the light was beginning to fade.

'I'm in a bit of a hurry,' I said. 'Is it something quick?'

Greg pouted. 'I've walked over specially, Kate. Can't I come in for a minute?'

This was terrible. You know what it's like when someone 'comes in for a minute'. You're lucky if they've gone an hour later. But how could I turn him away? OK, so he'd obviously been slagging me off left, right and centre but then I'd hit him, hadn't I? He had some excuse. And, if I was brutally honest, he could be forgiven for thinking I fancied him, seeing as I had danced with him all night at his party.

I dropped my bike on the path. 'Oh all right,' I said, trying desperately to sound gracious. 'But only for a minute, OK? I really do have to go.'

I took him in through the front door and showed him into the sitting room. It was a mess – baby toys lying around, the ironing board set up in front of the TV and a random pile of papers scattered on the sofa. Rover had sneaked in and was doing a pathetic job of hiding behind the sofa. When he saw Chloe and Biggles, he gave up and bounded forward excitedly, swiping the cord of the iron with his tail and sending it flying. Greg dropped the dog leads and leaped for it, cunningly catching it just before it hit the ground. He grinned triumphantly.

'Not bad, hey?' he said.

'Brilliant,' I agreed, taking it off him. 'Have a seat.' I shuffled the papers to one side. It wasn't exactly welcoming but I didn't want him to feel too comfortable.

'Back in a minute,' I said and shot through to the kitchen.

Only Belle was there. She was dyeing a top she didn't like.

'I was going to go over to talk to Chas but I can't because Greg's come round,' I announced. I had to tell someone.

'Oh Kate!' she said. 'That is bad. You will have to get rid of him.'

'I know,' I said. 'But how? I hit him – and he's walked all the way over here to see me.'

'You *could* say you will go on a date with him – just to make him happy. Then you could ring him later and say you have changed your mind.'

'You think that's why he's come? To ask me out again?'

Belle shrugged. 'For what other reason?' she said.

'But I can't say that!' I protested. 'It would be so... devious!'

Belle tossed back her hair. 'You have to be ruthless, Kate,' she said, looking pleased with the word. 'It is the only way.'

Ruthless. Great. Well, it might work for Belle but I couldn't see it working for me. I couldn't see Mum or Dad quoting any Bible verses at me about why I should be ruthless.

I went back to the sitting room and slowly opened the door. Greg was sitting nervously on the edge of the sofa, stroking each dog in turn.

'Sorry,' I said. 'Just something I needed to tell Belle. So why have you come over?'

Ouch! That sounded awful. So bald and well... ruthless. I leaned against the ironing board. 'I mean, it's really nice of you after what I did... I just wasn't expecting...'

Greg interrupted me. 'I came to say sorry,' he said. His cheeks were scarlet under the bruising. 'I shouldn't have grabbed you like that. I should have listened to what you said.'

'No,' I said, blushing furiously myself. 'I... I overreacted. It's me that should be apologizing. And I did rather hog you at your party... I could understand it if you thought...' It was too excruciatingly embarrassing. I couldn't go on.

'Yeah, but I've been slagging you off all day. That was just mean. It isn't your fault if you don't...'

'I do *like* you, Greg,' I butted in. 'It's just... well, it's just that, like I said...'

'I'm not your type?'

I shook my head.

'I can't change your mind on that?'

For a few seconds, I thought about it. Should I go out with him? Just give it a try? That would show Lisa – and Cute Carly and all the other girls who thought I was a bit of a loser. I was tempted, I'll admit it. But no, apart from anything else, it would be so unfair to Greg.

I shook my head again. 'No, Greg, I'm sorry. But thank you for coming over. I really appreciate it.' And I did, even though I was horribly aware of the minutes ticking by and the darkening sky.

'Oh well, it was worth a try.' Greg let out a long slow breath and stood up.

At that moment, Belle burst into the sitting room. She had changed out of her old dyeing-clothes outfit and looked fantastic in a skimpy top and tiny skirt.

'Oh,' she said. 'I am so sorry. I did not realize. I was going to take Rover for a walk.'

I gawked at her and she gave me a very odd look back. She turned smoothly to Greg.

'How lovely, Greg – you are here with your beautiful dogs!

Perhaps you would like to come with me?'

Then the penny dropped and I realized what she was up to. I could barely stop myself from bursting out laughing. Good old Belle. Not so Belladonna after all! Greg was blushing furiously.

'Ohh… er… that would be lovely,' he said. 'Err… I was just leaving, as it happens.'

'Perfect timing,' smiled Belle, winking at me as she stooped to clip on Rover's lead.

'Well, I'll go too, then,' I said. 'Thanks so much for coming over, Greg. I'll see you at school.' Then I bolted out of the house and leapt on my bike. Brilliant, Belle, I thought. *Boys always like me. I understand boys.* Well, she certainly did. And this time, it had been to my advantage.

As I cycled past the entrance to the park and started up the road that leads to Chas's farm, I began to feel uneasy. Surely the sky was darker than it should be at this time in the evening? The air was hot and sticky and my head was aching slightly. That could be down to tension – it had been a pretty stressful few days – but I suspected it was more to do with the weather. It didn't take a genius to guess that a storm was on its way.

I put more effort into cycling but it was hard. The road rises gradually and it was a real slog. Before long, my T-shirt was sticking to my back and I was wishing I had changed into shorts. Sweat was beginning to trickle down the sides of my face. Lovely! I would stink by the time I got there! But I wasn't going to turn back. I was terrified that if I didn't make myself speak to Chas tonight, I never would.

Suddenly, a breeze seemed to spring up from nowhere. The trees which lined the road rustled and heaved, lifting their branches as if they were waving at me. The sudden gust of air was refreshing but I knew what it meant; it was the edge of the storm. Any moment now, the rain would come. Sure enough, there was flash and then an angry grumble from up ahead. Great! I was cycling into it.

Come on, I told myself. Come on. It's only another mile or so. I was leaving the trees behind. Another mile or so didn't seem very appealing on an exposed road across open countryside. A second flash outlined the distant hills, more thunder rumbled and then down came the rain.

It was so sudden and heavy that I jammed on my brakes with the shock and nearly swerved out in front of a car that was just behind me. It passed with a blare of horn. (Question: why do people blow their horns, *after* you've made a mistake? I mean, you don't need anyone to rub it in – you feel like a complete idiot anyway!)

I stopped to recover myself and peered up the hill through the driving rain. Water was already pouring down each side of the road in sudden, brand new streams, just where a cyclist needs to cycle. The drops were so big and heavy that it was difficult to see the way forward. I was soaked through. Should I turn back? But Chas's farm was closer than home. I would press on, pushing my bike. A downpour like this couldn't last too long.

Wrong. It could and it did. Thunder roared and lightning

flashed almost incessantly. That's what it felt like anyway. I was getting quite scared. Do you know that fewer people are murdered each year by strangers than are struck by lightning? That's supposed to be comforting – like you're not very likely to be murdered by a stranger. It just makes me worried about being struck by lightning.

The road began to flatten out and I got back on my bike. I had this feeling that I would be safer on it because of the rubber tyres. And, so long as I was careful, I thought I would be quicker too. It wasn't far now, I knew.

A Land Rover was approaching, headlights full on in the gloom. It slowed to a stop opposite me. Mr Peterson wound down the window.

'Kate, put your bike in the back,' he called. 'Chas was getting worried about you.'

Chas, almost unrecognizable in heavy waterproofs, had already leaped out and grabbed my handle bars.

'I'll do it,' he said. 'You get in.'

'The back?' I queried. I was so wet, I would have drenched the front seats.

'Probably best,' he said.

I ran across the road and scrambled into the car. Chas shoved my bike in, climbed in himself and slammed the door.

'OK Dad, Thunderbirds are go,' he said and shot me a nervous grin.

We didn't speak on the short journey up to the farm. It would have been difficult to hear each other above the drumming of the rain on the roof and the crashing of the thunder. When we arrived in the yard, Mrs Peterson flung open the door and hurried out with a huge umbrella.

'Your dad was on the phone, Kate,' she said. 'He wanted to know if you'd got here before the storm. I'll ring him back now.' She tried to hand the umbrella over to me but her husband stopped her.

'Kate's soaked anyway,' he said. 'You go inside.'

'But...'

'Don't argue,' Mr Peterson barked, to my absolute astonishment. He's always such a mild, quiet, softly spoken man. Mrs Charming tends to do the talking for both of them.

But she didn't argue. When Chas took me in through the side door, she was already on the phone.

'Want a shower?' Chas asked.

I nodded. My teeth were chattering too much to talk.

'Look, I'll bring you Mum's bathrobe,' he said. 'Then you can leave your wet stuff in here.'

I nodded again and hoped he'd be quick.

Standing in the Petersons' power shower a few minutes later, hot water pounding onto my head, it was difficult to think. Having got here, how was I going to start? What was I going to say? How could I explain without sounding like a pathetic, snivelling, jealous little brat? The shower was lovely; I stayed in it until Chas hammered on the door.

'I've put some of my clothes out here for you,' he shouted. 'When you're ready, do you want to come over to the den?'

'Yes!' I yelled back.

Well, this was it then. I turned off the shower reluctantly and stepped out onto the thick velvety mat. The towels were huge and soft and fluffy, a far cry from the ones we have at home. Arrayed along the sill were expensive lotions and potions. Floris, Crabtree and Evelyn, Molton Brown – names which would never cross the threshold in our house. Mrs Charming had always seemed the most unlikely friend for my mum but they got on really well. So what was wrong? Just the fact that it had been Chas ushering me to the shower and bringing me clothes spoke volumes. That was the sort of job Mrs Charming normally relished.

Chas is skinny but tall so I had to roll up the bottoms of the jeans he'd put out. The T-shirt and hoody didn't fit too badly and I found a brush with a matching comb and mirror so I quickly dealt with my hair. Oh well, Chas had seen me look worse. It was now or never.

The rain had slackened off as the storm passed so I made a quick barefoot dash across the yard, hauling up Chas's jeans still further. I hesitated at the door of the den, wondering if I really dared to go in. The last time I had been here had been so awful. Then I took a deep breath, whispered a brief prayer (see? I'm getting better – I remembered!) and flung the door open.

Chas was making hot chocolate. Various cats were draped decoratively about the place. The mess didn't seem to have moved. Maybe we could just rewind and pretend the rows had never happened.

Chas stood up, offered me a mug and raised his eyebrows.

I gulped nervously.

'I don't know what to say, Chas,' I said. 'Everyone says I should talk to you but I don't know what to say.'

Silence. I couldn't look Chas in the eyes so I found myself staring at his slim, brown neck. Very Johnny Depp. I gave myself a mental shake. That wasn't what I was there for.

'Well?' said Chas. 'Are you going to take this mug off me or have I got to stand here for the rest of my life?'

I took the mug. 'Err... thank you,' I said.

Chas gestured at the old sofa. 'Want a seat?' he said. It was clear of its usual heaps of odds and ends; he'd obviously made an effort to tidy up for me.

'Err... thanks,' I said. My legs were distinctly wobbly; I was glad to sit down. Chas plonked himself next to me. In the past, I would have sat back or even sprawled out on the sofa. Today, I perched on the edge sipping my hot chocolate. So, I noticed, did Chas. I tried out various opening lines in my head. 'I just wanted to say I'm really sorry...' No, why should I say sorry first? 'Chas, please tell me what's wrong?' No, too direct. 'Look, I know it's none of my business, but what's going on between you and Lisa?' No – because it really was none of my business. I had nearly drunk all my hot chocolate. Panic! What was I going to do? I had to say something!

'Chas...'

'Kate...'

We stopped, laughed nervously and for the first time in ages our eyes met.

'You first,' said Chas.

149

'No, you…' I said.

Chas shook his head firmly. It was down to me then. I took a deep breath.

'Chas,' I said, 'what's wrong with your mum?'

There! I'd said it. Having just seen her, that was the question at the forefront of my mind. It was a start at any rate.

Chas looked at me. To my horror, I could see that his hands were trembling. I took his mug off him quickly.

'What is it, Chas?' I gasped. 'What's the matter?'

'I wanted to tell you,' Chas mumbled, 'but Mum wanted to keep it a secret. Your mum knows. She's the only one apart from me and Dad.'

'Know what? Your mum… she's not… she's not dying or something, is she?' I said, my heart suddenly beginning to pound so hard that my chest hurt.

Chas shook his head and I felt my shoulders sag with relief. 'The doctors don't think so – not now. They think they caught it in time.'

They think they caught it in time. That only ever meant one thing.

'Cancer?' I said. I felt sick. It wasn't just the thought of the illness; it was the fact that I'd been so mean when Chas must have been feeling dreadful. I'd even justified not praying for him because he wasn't going to church! My cheeks burned with shame.

Chas nodded. 'She's been having treatment. An operation. Then radiotherapy. It's made her so tired and run down – like a different person.'

Everything suddenly made sense. 'I'm *so* sorry, Chas,' I said. 'I wish I'd known. I never thought... I mean, her hair's fine and everything. I just thought...' No, I didn't want to tell him what I'd thought. How insulting! All the time poor Mrs C had been really poorly and I'd been thinking she was on the point of divorce!

'Idiot,' Chas said. 'It's chemotherapy, not radiotherapy that makes your hair drop out.'

'I'm sorry... I didn't know... but they... they've said she's going to be OK?

'Yes... yes... they think so. She still feels rough but she's getting better. I know, I should be all right, shouldn't I? Not blithering on like this. It's not me that's ill. But I feel awful. I mean, you never know with cancer, do you?'

'No.' That sounded terrible. Desperately, I fished around for something comforting to say. 'But they've said they think she'll be OK. That's got to be good, hasn't it?'

'Yeah, yeah, I know. I just... well, I just can't bear to think about it... that she might die. I mean, I know she's a pain in the butt a lot of the time but... well...'

'I know,' I said. 'That's how I felt when Mum fractured her skull. It was such a shock. I suddenly realized how much I cared about her really.'

'Yeah, well, I couldn't face it – or anyone else. I just kept going off on my own. And then I was kicking around down the park one night and one of the lads let me have a go on his board.'

'His skateboard?'

'Yeah.' Chas turned to me, his eyes suddenly alight. I realized how long it had been seen I'd seen him look like that. 'And I could do it!' he continued. 'I couldn't believe it. I mean, it just seemed easy to me. They were all raving on about how I was a natural and honestly, Kate – you'd never believe the buzz that gave me, especially when I was feeling so bad. It felt fantastic after years of being a bit of an outsider. It's not like they talk to you about anything except skateboarding, of course. But that was great too – not having to face it. When you're skating you can't concentrate on anything else. You're always thinking about the next stunt – doing the last one better, finding the next rail or wall or whatever.'

'You do seem obsessed,' I agreed.

'Yeah… well… maybe I am. It's really addictive. You should try it, Kate!'

I laughed. 'Maybe I will,' I said. 'At least I might see more of you then.'

There was an awkward silence.

'Sorry,' I said. 'I know it wasn't just you…'

'No, it was,' said Chas. 'Well, mainly. I just couldn't explain. Mum wanted it kept secret and I felt weird… kind of numb and angry at the same time.'

I nodded. 'Angry that it had happened?' I said. 'Like, "Why *my* mum? What did *she* ever do wrong?" That's how I felt when Mum had her accident.'

'Yes, like that. But angry with Mum too, I don't know why. Even angry with you. I wanted you to… I don't know… just magically understand or something. It was like I was stuck in this awful tunnel. There was nothing but worrying about Mum and skateboarding and computer games. I couldn't go to church; I couldn't pray. I had to keep my mind busy all the time or I panicked and felt sick. If I tired myself out with skateboarding, I could sleep. If I didn't, I just lay there and worried.'

'I can see why you didn't come to Gran's funeral now,' I said quietly.

Chas winced. 'I feel terrible about that. I really liked your gran, honestly. I would have come, I should have come – but I just couldn't face it. Dad couldn't either. We were wimps. Mum went, of course.'

Of course. 'She's amazing, your mum,' I said.

Chas smiled wryly. 'I know,' he said. 'I never really realized before.'

Feeling very bold because I've never done it before, I put my hand on Chas's knee. 'I'm sorry I've been so foul to you,' I said.

'Stop saying "sorry",' Chas said. 'It wasn't your fault. That day when Rover ate my skateboard wax. I was horrible to you – but I just couldn't handle anything. Then I lost my temper and you left and it's all been awful ever since. Just after the funeral when I met Belle and came back to your house… I wanted to sort it out then but you were so angry.'

'Gran had just died. I wasn't…'

'I know, I know, I was stupid, it wasn't your fault.'

'No, no, it wasn't your fault either.'

Maybe it was mentioning Gran, I don't know, but suddenly I was choked with tears and then, just as suddenly Chas had his arms round me and I was crying on his shoulder, finally letting go of all the weeks of stress and misery. It wasn't exciting or romantic or embarrassing – just a huge, huge, relief. Like coming home.

'But your mum *is* getting better, Chas,' I said, at last, sitting back and blowing my nose. 'It all could have been much worse.'

Chas scrubbed his face with his sleeve. So he'd been crying too. 'Yes, I know. That's the only reason I can tell you all this. I don't think she'll mind now – and anyway, I couldn't bear it any longer. Do you think I'm a real wimp?'

'Don't be silly!' I said. 'She shouldn't have kept it a secret. People would have helped. People would have prayed.'

Chas shook his head. 'She couldn't bear the thought of people ringing her up and asking how she was. I know she's all loud and jolly most of the time but in some ways she's a really private person. It's weird, isn't it? People are such a mixture. Sometimes she drives me crazy and other times I can't imagine life without her. But then I think that about a lot of people.'

'That's exactly what I think,' I said. 'I keep worrying that I don't really love anyone at all. There's *nobody* who doesn't irritate me some of the time. Do you think I just don't meet the right people?'

Chas shook his head. ''Course not. It's just that loving people is more difficult than you think. That's why there's that great long list in the Bible about love being patient and kind and not giving up and so on – because half the time, you *want* to give up!'

'Oh not that bit,' I groaned. 'Mum gave me that on a really tacky card. The trouble is, I can't get it out of my head. D'you know what else it says?'

'Not much. Why?'

'It says "Love is not jealous". How stupid is that?'

Chas pulled a face. 'Well, I guess if you really loved someone, you'd want them to be happy – so you wouldn't be jealous if...'

'But *I'm* jealous,' I burst out. Suddenly I couldn't hold it in any longer. 'I'm jealous that you spend so much time skateboarding, I'm jealous because you've got a bunch of new friends, I'm jealous because of the way you look at Belle and I'm jealous because you kissed Lisa. And it doesn't mean I don't want you to be happy – it just means...'

I paused. What was I going to say? That I didn't want him to be happy without me? How selfish was that? If you really cared about someone, you couldn't be jealous. You had to let them be free, let them live their own life – even if you got hurt. If you hung onto them, jealousy really was like a monster that would you eat you up – and that would hurt even worse.

'Oh *Lisa*,' Chas interrupted. 'That was so stupid. I was in this "what the heck" kind of mood, I was so depressed. Lisa's always hanging around me – never gives up, you know she doesn't. I just kind of gave in to the pressure. Why not? I was past caring. Mistake. She reeked of stale booze and cigarette smoke. Yuk. Forget it. That's history. And Belle – well, of course I fancy her! Any boy would – but I'm not so stupid as to get serious about her!'

I didn't say anything. I couldn't. This huge flood of relief was washing over me. Chas was still the same person – he was still the friend who understood me the best. He didn't like Lisa or Belle better than me. He'd just been, as he said himself, stuck in a tunnel for a while.

'Penny for them,' said Chas.

'What?' I said, dazed.

'Penny for your thoughts. What are you frowning so hard about?'

I smiled. 'I was just thinking about Mum,' I said. 'How she usually turns out to be right in the end. Very irritating really.'

'Like my mum,' Chas agreed. 'I feel bad about it but it still drives me mad when she keeps on at me to clear up.'

'She's hoping that one day she'll turn you into a tidy person,' I said.

'No chance' said Chas, sweeping his eyes around his den.

'Yeah, well *you* know that and *I* know that but she still has her dreams,' I said. 'Love never gives up remember?'

I picked up the empty mugs.

'Can I make some more hot chocolate?' I asked.

'Of course.' Chas reached for the kettle. 'Kate, you nearly gave up on me this time, didn't you?' he said. 'And I nearly gave up on you.'

'Never again,' I said. 'I hope.'

156

'Me too,' he said. 'Now give me those mugs.'

I passed them over.

'I've just thought of something!' I gasped. I'd suddenly remembered the bet I had with Ben. Ten pounds that Mr and Mrs Peterson were about to divorce. Rats, I'd well and truly lost it. Served me right.

'What?' demanded Chas.

'I owe Ben a tenner!' I said.

'Why?'

'Oh, it doesn't matter,' I said. 'It's a long story.' I smiled. I was too happy to have my best friend back again to care about the money.

'Kate,' said Chas suddenly. 'D'you think we're going to go on like this for ever?'

'How d'you mean?'

'Rowing and making up. It was Carly, then it was Nic, then it was me going away to school...'

'And the dog,' I interrupted.

'Yes, and now it's skateboarding and Belle and Lisa.'

'Well, your mum being ill and Gran dying didn't exactly help,' I said.

'Yes, I know but... well... d'you think we could... well... *not* give each other such a hard time? I mean, whoever I fancy or whatever's going on, I'm never really happy if I've rowed with you.'

'Me too,' I said. 'And I panic that you've stopped liking me. I never expect people to like me very much.'

'Well, I do,' said Chas. 'I always have.'

157

'I wasn't fishing for compliments,' I said, embarrassed.

'I know you weren't,' said Chas.

Our eyes met and I knew that something had changed in our friendship – something I'd suspected might happen for a long time – and I needed time to think and to pray. This wasn't the moment to act first and think later; for once, that was obvious. Vicky would be proud of me – and so would Mum, of course.

Maybe Chas thought the same.

'It's getting late,' he said. 'The rain's stopped. Look, it's a lovely evening out there now. Want me to cycle back home with you?'

I smiled in delight. 'That would be just brilliant,' I said.

All Lion books are available from your local bookshop, or can be ordered via our website or from Marston Book Services. For a free catalogue, showing the complete list of titles available, please contact:

Customer Services
Marston Book Services
PO Box 269
Abingdon
Oxon
OX14 4YN

Tel:01235 465500
Fax: 01235 465555

Our website can be found at:
www.lionhudson.com